PAGE

PASSAGE

***

PAGE

PASSAGE

A Literary Novel by

DANIEL HILL ZAFREN

Published by Time Treasures Books, West Jefferson, North Carolina

ISBN 13: 978-0-9833042-2-7

Printed in the United States of America

Cover and interior design by Susan Newman Design Inc.

Earlier captivating works by this often-praised author are listed below. Each is distinct and presents significant life lessons in an interesting setting with memorable characters.

In a World We Never Made (2001)
A Door Never Opened (2003)
Shadow Selves (2005)
Network of Death (2006)
Not Lost – Just Not Found (2008)
Restless Beauty (2009)
Glimpses of Forgotten Dreams (2010)
Echo in the Heart (2011)
Double Hugs (2011)

www.timetreasuresbooks.com

This is an insightful story about writers and writing. It attempts to capture the essence of the glory of the written word as it is strung along to create passages on the page that are memorable as a lasting impression on the reader. It embraces the struggles of a writer to bring that magic to full force. It is hoped that this meaningful story will inspire and motivate the reader to write.

Every person's story is a page from life. A novelist collects and arranges those pages using imagination as the transport for the hopeful journey to a satisfying and thoughtful destination, a poignant passage. Events and characters, imaginary or to some degree real, are threaded through the segments of the written word to help produce the profound, tickle the fancy or lead thoughts and feelings to places memorable and significant. Ongoing deliberations and numerous rewrites set a true and definite course for the excursion.

In a good book, it is thrilling to anticipate what passage the next page will bring. Likewise, it can be exciting and challenging to discover what the next page in our life story will contain. It is sage advice in writing to create one page at a time. It is equally valid to proceed with our life story one page at a time.

Writing can open new vistas. Writing is the vessel to cross the sea of dreams to lands yet undiscovered. As opposed to the difficulty in the real life in which one stumbles through, a writer has the invigorating opportunity to redo what is written before such can be challenged. The written word can be refined as many times as needed to usher in the comfort and satisfaction of its creator. It is a noble and worthwhile endeavor that necessarily involves and consumes the whole person. It is that person. It can be no other way.

A word is a bud attempting to become a twig.
How can one not dream while writing? It is
the pen which dreams. The blank page gives
the right to dream.

Gaston Bachelard

All good books are alike in that they are truer than if they had really happened and after you have finished reading one you will feel that all that happened to you and afterwards it all belongs to you; the good and the bad, the ecstasy, the remorse and the sorrow, the people and the places and how the weather was. If you can get so that you can give that to people, then you are a writer.

Ernest Hemingway

ONE

The dual concept of writing as a magical journey along with the challenge of creating segments of words that identify closely with the current of life lingered with him. He looked from the lone window of the small office over the broad expanse of lawns comprising the campus quadrangle of Blantyre University in New England. Holding one of the finest academic reputations in the nation, Blantyre was also a legend in the annals of professor and student involvement in societal upheavals. At the time of the university protests in the late 1960s and early 1970s, a number of the teachers at Blantyre were infamous in radical traditions and activity. A noteworthy student uprising at the school took place well after campus unrest elsewhere had quieted down. Stories were rampant of professors and students rising and falling as idols and hapless victims of those volatile times. Even today their lives are still the topic of animated conversations in dormitories, fraternity and sorority houses, and teacher lounges. One professor who had become a scapegoat at the time captured it all in a book still widely read today.

Professor of Creative Writing was an impressive description. Connor Chase was not sure he did the right thing by taking on this role. Yet, it seemed to be a logical next step in the progression of his writing career. After four favorably reviewed novels, even if sales were disappointing considering most reader approval, he had garnered enough of a respected reputation to be asked as a guest speaker at book festivals and other literary events. This teaching offer came without any solicitation on his part. He would be teaching a freshman class in creative writing two times a week and one weekly graduate seminar in fiction production aptly described as a workshop. This did not seem to be a demanding schedule so as to detract from his pursuits. There should be ample time to work on his fifth novel, which, at the moment, was not even a mental seed.

He stared at the manicured lawns, the shrubbery, and the majestic mountains in the distance. A brisk wind swayed the trees as if producing a life force for them. Today was his thirtieth birthday. His parents had called him earlier in the day from the retirement community in North Carolina where they had recently settled. Computer messages and cards from friends, mostly writer acquaintances, topped off the acknowledgement of the day.

His most recent romantic involvement had ended shortly before he left for Blantyre. Even if promising in the beginning, none of these relationships had ripened into a time-tested satisfaction and value. Perhaps, much of this was his fault. He quickly grew bored, and he would erect a form of barrier to discourage further involvement.

He liked people but long ago discovered he did not need them. Not being content with ordinary qualities in people was a stark weakness on his part, and he was powerless or lacked the incentive to overcome it. Perhaps it was more the underlying haunting by a ghost memory. Maybe it was also the writer in him. There certainly were common characters in his books, and in that form he accepted that people need not be exceptional to be interesting or noteworthy. Yet, he would find some means to propel them or instill in them a quality or event that would raise them to prominence. It was as if he had impatience with most people and was stymied in not bringing such a distinction to them as to keep his attention and an ongoing interest. It was a barrier to his happiness and a source of frustration. He could not control himself in his life story almost as if he was stuck on the same page over and over again.

On this thirtieth birthday, maybe it was an opportune time to take stock of his life. That meant a review of where he had been and where he was going. He had to define the person he was and the person he wanted to be. He had done that for the characters in his books, a relatively simple task compared to doing it for himself.

One of the first meaningful moments he remembered, meaningful in the sense that his thinking went beyond the normal confines of his day-to-day routine and wants, was looking out of the window from the small tenement apartment his family lived in on Manhattan's East Side and that overlooked a portion of the East River. It was a shabby old building and the windows were ill fit and drafty. Yet, they were large by contemporary standards and this provided an expansive view of the water and the numerous varying boats that sailed up and down. What would it be like to be on one of those ships? To what exotic or mysterious places had they been to or to where they were going? For a youngster whose life was geared to the confined existence of life in the surrounding streets, the possibilities staggered his imagination. The river too was a source of wonderment to a mind that seemed to have no bounds. Its color changed as if it had moods of its own. It had to be there long before people settled along it. Why would the river want that? Why did it allow it?

His father had a clerical job with the sanitation department, and his mother gave piano lessons on the old spinet in the living room. There was only one bedroom, and he slept on a pullout bed in the hallway between the kitchen and the living room. The sounds of classical music, mostly piano masterpieces filled the air from the old victrola. He was taught to play the piano and did fairly well at it, but it did not hold the attention and fascination that writing represented once he was introduced to the flying pen. He had not sat at a keyboard for many years and did not miss it, although he knew his mother was disappointed.

For several summers, he went to a children's camp in Connecticut. His mother would take him by subway to Grand Central Station where the campers would congregate for the train ride to the town near the camp. Buses would then take them the rest of the way.

He never fully enjoyed the camp and was constantly frustrated at having to go to activities according to a strict schedule. Yet, there were experiences and sensations that stayed with him and became an inner reservoir of feelings and understandings. He learned about and appreciated the nuances of nature, and still could recall the contrast between a country environment and the sounds of a city. He learned to swim, to be an archer, and to play tennis. The letters he wrote to his parents were probably the initial introduction into the world of writing. Each letter was long and filled with detailed descriptions of what he did and his reactions to them.

It was at the camp that he kissed his first girl, Marilyn Cornstock, who lived on Long Island. He would never forget her name and the freckles that seemed to blink at him. He had been aware she would stare at him from the girl's side of the dining room, and when his eyes would meet her gaze a smile would acknowledge a special communication. One rainy day, he went to the camp director's office to mail a letter to his parents and she was there doing the same thing. They talked for a moment and she said for him to come with her behind the office as she wanted to show him something. He could still remember the sound of the rain on her umbrella as she leaned into him and kissed him on the lips. Instinctively, he kissed her back enthralled by the warm and soft feeling of her full lips. They hatched a secret code, and for the rest of the summer they would meet behind the office often and experimented with variations of kissing. They exchanged letters for a few months after that until she stopped writing. She was not at the camp the following summer.

They had no car, and he could not remember his frugal parents ever going away or even having a vacation in those early years. He went to public school and struggled through a mediocre education. He was a loner in elementary school, and his only two friends were two older boys in the building where he lived. They hung out together, and between their tutelage and the lessons of the streets he was a keen observer and quick reactor to all that went on around him.

He had a girlfriend in high school. This pretty girl with long jet-black hair and piercing black eyes who was in his homeroom and several of his other classes kept staring at him just as Marilyn had at the camp. Her interest in him was returned two-fold. They started talking, then dated, and went to classes or down the school hallways always holding hands. She led him to read more and they would read aloud to each other. Dorie Stein was Jewish and while his parents were not crazy about the idea of him dating a Jewish girl steadily they never made a major issue out of it. Actually, they grew quite fond of her as her soft-spoken and courteous mannerism was beguiling. Dorie lived five blocks away in a cramped apartment with four siblings. Each time he went there to pick her up he was amazed at the chaos that abounded in such a restrictive space.

Dorie was more than a sweetheart. She entrenched herself as his best friend and an alter ego. She wrote ever-flowing poetry as a display of an imagination that had wings. He wrote short stories, and they delighted in the reading to one another of their creations. He was mesmerized by her poems, reflective of a human depthness well beyond his comprehension at the time. The first time they made love he had taken her to his apartment while his parents were at Lincoln Center for a piano concert. The souls of the writer and the poet were intertwined and both agreed that their creative efforts gained added fervor.

Every Saturday morning they would take the subway to Union Square and spend the day rummaging through the seemingly endless carts of used books on the sidewalk in front of the many bookstores. Dorie would hold up any volume of poetry that caught her fancy and would read aloud a portion in his ear. They would share a sandwich from a delicatessen. Dorie had introduced him to a corned beef or pastrami sandwich on seeded rye bread. They would not let go of hand holding, even while eating. Tired by the end of the day, she would rest her head on his shoulder during the subway ride back home. Those were times filled with a secret contentment. It was an introduction to one of the amazing attributes of humanity and love – the sharing of thoughts is a powerful and lasting pleasure. Strong feelings can accentuate the smallest victory. Peaceful moments can be a prelude to an extended time of satisfaction.

They loved the old movies, especially the silent ones. Whenever one of the offbeat cinemas held a Charlie Chaplin festival, they would sit through multiple showings of the films laughing so hard as if they were taking them in for the first time. Her caresses were nonstop and emotional outpourings spontaneous. The darkened theater fostered multiple emphatic kisses.

Each time he left her at her apartment there was an emotional drop. The last goodnight kiss would be accompanied by her tears indicating not an ending but an unwarranted interruption. He could taste the salt from the tears on his lips after breaking away from the final embrace. It was as if one of her poems and one of his stories were unfinished.

Midway in their junior year, the Steins bought a house in New Jersey so the family could have sufficient room to develop. Connor suspected that one additional reason unstated was a wariness of the growing seriousness of Dorie's relationship with a boy who was not Jewish. Despite tearful declarations and earnest vows, the relationship faded away and they lost contact. He still had the shoebox filled with scraps of paper her poems were scribbled on. Every once and awhile he would open the box and the warm memories would flood in leaving him wondering about what might have been or even what should have been.

His parents had saved enough through a long struggled life to send him to college. They knew he wanted to be a writer, and they supported his desire even though they secretly wished he would choose a more financially promising avenue.

He spent four years at Columbia University saving expenses by living at home. Any dates he had were disappointing as that poignant recollection of Dorie raised defeating comparisons. He finished his first novel and it was published in his senior year. As some royalties trickled in he rented a small apartment in Greenwich Village knowing he needed a quiet place to work and not be subject to distractions at home.

There he remained, doing three more books and living in the shadows of a novelist. The world appeared in the abstract and major challenges arose as he continually struggled to come out into the light. Brooding discontent was broken up by book tours and guest appearances at book festivals, and as long as he did not have to deal strictly with himself he coasted along waiting for an event to recharge his spirit and to brighten his outlook. Would this teaching adventure be his life path?

[T]he ideal novel that deeply stirs everyone will never be written

Scott Turow

Writing is . . . a series of permissions you give yourself to be expressive in certain ways. To invent. To leap. To fall. To find your own characteristic way of narrating and insisting, that is, to find your own inner freedom.

Susan Sontag

There are loyal hearts, there are spirits brave,
There are souls that are pure and true;
Then give to the world the best you have,
And the best will come back to you.

Mary Ainge De Vere

***

TWO

At the first session of the freshman class, he scanned the youthful faces of the twenty-seven students. He surmised each had a different reason for being there. Some may have estimated it would be an easy class because there was no required textbook. Others may have varying desires or curiosity about becoming a writer. He even ventured to guess that at least one harbored a long-standing dream of writing a famous book. That had been his dream from the first short story he wrote when he was twelve. That story was not good and he never showed it to anyone. Yet, it made him feel a sense of power to accomplish setting his thoughts down on paper. He relished the challenge of creating a beginning, the excitement of finding an ending, and the satisfaction in building a bridge between the two.

"So, you want to be a writer? Hopefully, here you will learn how to write. Why you want to write is your personal demon. It will not be an easy road to travel, and unless you have a strong motivation I suggest this class will not be for you. There will be much writing, strenuous at best. One cannot write without reading, and you will be doing a great deal of that, too. There is no text for this course, but before you leave I will give you an extensive reading list. All of the materials are on reserve at the library, and many can be found on line. These readings will give you an insight into how others write, what they write, and why they write."

Connor paced back and forth at the front of the class before he resumed speaking. "You may think it is not a question of what you have to say but how you say it. Actually, it is a combination of both. Experience and imagination are the major components, and how they interact can make an ordinary event entertaining and meaningful. There may not be any set formula to follow, and more of one may be needed in a particular situation. Underlying it all is the virtue of patience. One needs to be tolerant of the dry moments and to understand that frustration is normal when progress appears nonexistent and the end product is deemed unworthy. It can take many years to write a book. It may take a lifetime. It may never reach fruition."

He resumed the pacing. "Another aspect of writing is that it is a solitary activity unless part of a collaborative effort. Outside distractions, whether physical or emotional, can be highly disturbing. This can be overwhelming when one has a family, a job, and an assortment of hobbies or other involvements. Writers may have to do a juggling act with a vast array of daily demands. The solitary nature of writing can heat up tempers and cause friction when other people and events demand your time and attention. It can usher in unintended and hurtful consequences. At the least, most authors are thought of as eccentric. All of this is said not to dissuade you from writing or to scare you. It is just a dose of reality to confront. As each person is different so is the action or reaction to a writing and the person who writes it. Moments can be easy or a monumental strain, or at any point along the extended line that reaches between the two extremes. Is it worth the effort, the possible torment? That is the million-dollar question. For each of you, the answer will only come after a genuine attempt to do it. Only each of you can decide not only whether or not you can write but also whether you have the heart and soul of a writer."

He broke away from the oratory to take the attendance, asking the students to correct the pronunciation of their names if necessary. Sixteen females and eleven males, all young and seemingly bright and attentive. He wondered whether there would be ample fuel to ignite a fire of creativity.

"Let's try a little exercise. I will give you a sentence and part of the next sentence. You complete it. There was the sound of breaking glass behind him. He ……. Anyone wish to continue with the narrative?"

A woman with straight brown hair and glasses offered, "He was startled."

"That is part of a thought. He was startled and what……peed in his pants"?

The students laughed. A man in a tan turtleneck sweater spoke up. "He was startled and turned around to see what had happened."

"Redundant. If he turned around, he would see what happened."

A woman in the front row, a red bow in her hair, added, "He turned around and could not believe what he saw."

"That does raise interest and anticipation. That is what you want to accomplish. Yet, you could just say he could not believe what he saw. Turning around would be implied since it took place behind him. Now, once you have raised a level of anticipation, you do not want to disappoint the reader. It would be a letdown to say that a woman was picking up the broken pieces of the mirror from her compact. If you promise something, you have to try and deliver. Any ideas?"

A woman in the rear of the class wearing sunglasses broke a brief silence. "How about the car crash was more extensive than he thought it might be."

"If that was the case, he would have heard more than breaking glass. There would have been crushing metal and perhaps even a blaring horn and screams. Observations and conclusions have to be plausible." The room was quiet. With no further offerings from the student mass, he continued. "How about he saw there were broken pieces of a large mirror scattered around on the sidewalk and not another person was around. That prompts a bit of a mystery while establishing the reason for the noise. The bottom line is that writing should be concise, logical and prompt the reader to want to read on. Writing is a true art form. It may be natural to some of us, but for most it is a struggle. It takes experience and protracted thought. It is the result of a harvest of ideas and writing that reflects those ideas in style and sense."

He distributed the reading list that contained the reading selections and the dates for the readings to be completed by. "You will find that many writers in describing their undertakings detail the process as a turmoil, blood-letting, and an obsession. And, as with the old movie title, which you probably never heard of, it is a magnificent obsession. Try to feel the pain. If you are serious about wanting to write, you will want to taste the passion and will sympathize with their madness. Besides the reading, prepare for the next class a paragraph selecting what you think is your strongest personality trait and explain why it is so."

As he watched the students leave the room, he wondered how many would drop the course. It would be better for them and for him if they did that if the will to plod ahead was lacking.

Writing is a socially acceptable form of schizophrenia.

E. L. Doctorow

Why do writers write? Because it isn't there.

Thomas Berger

O World. Those choosest not the better part!
It is not wisdom to be only wise,
And on the inward vision close the eyes,
But it is wisdom to believe the heart.

George Santayana

***

THREE

She stared at the cover of her newest novel, the fifth revolving around the enigmatic detective heroine, Bailey Farrel.

A DISTANT CRY
by
Celia Ehnson

She loved the cover, just as she loved all of the earlier ones, each from a painting specifically done for the book by her best friend, Becca Ehrand. Each was engaging and thought-provoking. This one fully captured the rural farm scene where the strange disappearance of the teenage girl had taken place. Even the horses the girl rode were depicted in the painting.

Bailey Farrel took full advantage of her name, knowing full well that most people would expect a man to be the detective until they met her. An unexpected event can loosen tongues or otherwise alter behavior in the wake of a surprise. Celia used that technique in each story.

Because of the closeness in their names, the girls had their school desks next to each other throughout their school years. They were the same age and grew up a few blocks from one another. They were friends from the time of their early discovery of each other, and the closeness was sealed from that moment. They even developed special nicknames because of the nearly identical last names. They combined the first two letters of their first names with the first letter of their last names. Becca became Bee, and Celia was Cee. Bee married her high school sweetheart right after graduation and had two children, a boy, Evan, and a girl, Molly. Bee kept her maiden name since she had already developed as an artist and her paintings were always signed B. Ehrand. The paintings had been initially displayed and sold at Frank Johnson's general store in the small town in which they lived in North Carolina. The town was on the scenic route folks took on trips to the mountains, and many would stop at the store as the one convenient resting place with a quaint form of tourist attraction as well as the gas pumps to fill up their automobiles. The paintings sold well as Bee had a particular knack for portraying pastoral scenes with vibrant colors. Eventually, Bee built her own retail gallery and studio near the general store, and besides her paintings in the store people were directed to the nearby studio.

Cee, not nearly as attractive as Bee, dated rarely in high school and had no steady boyfriends. She never married, and now at the age of thirty-nine the prospects were dimming. Her mother had died twelve years ago, and she lived in that family home which was a few houses down from Bee and her family. After a much earlier divorce, Cee's father had gone his separate way and was never heard from again. Due to the closeness, Becca's family became her extended grouping. Being an honorary mother, Evan and Molly had an additional adult nurturing them in their growing years. The children affectionately addressed her as Momma Cee.

Since the friends lived so close, the two women would converse intimately and without any reserve. Even their moments of silence permeated with the warmth of congeniality, true sisters of the heart. Celia had all of the paintings Becca had done for the book covers, and she proudly displayed them on the walls of her home. Cee knew even if the remote opportunity arose for her to leave, she could never be far from Bee and the family. She also felt an endearing closeness to Len, Bee's attentive husband. Her heart reiterated the message she frequently inserted in her books that one must hold on to the dreams and blessings one has. For now, dreams were realized through Bailey's adventures, whether they were romantic or sleuth related.

It was a warm autumn day, and the leaves were just showing the first tinge of colors. Celia sat on the terrace just outside the kitchen, her Yorkshire terrier, Sherlock, resting in his customary warm spot across her lap. With pen in hand she wrote a few lines in the new Bailey saga, *The Ghost of the Mountain*. She had never considered the lack of a college education to be a detriment to her writing style or content. The unbounded imagination whisked her along to ever changing scenarios and into the depths of the minds of the characters. She never considered the nonuse of large or obscure words a negative aspect to her writings. In fact, she had always considered obfuscation an impediment to her enjoyment of reading. It was an unnecessary burden to come across a word that is unfamiliar and the meaning is not apparent by its context. Having to put the book aside and look up the definition was an unwelcome interruption in the flow of the story. Her radical thoughts reached far beyond the writings she pursued. It was her belief that a creative mind has many navigable tributaries.

The heart-warming morning ritual that launched their day was coffee at Bee's house after the children had left for school and Len had gone to his job at the post office. After that, Becca would go to her shop and studio and Celia would return to her writing at home. They would sit at the kitchen table and sip the coffee, often nibbling on some pastry that either lady had baked. They both were believers that a sweet morsel for the tongue in loving company brightens the moment and endures for the day. If the weather was especially pleasant, as it was this warm autumn morning, they would sit on the back porch in rockers. The conversation jumped around to numerous topics, ranging from general philosophical ideas to the intimate revelations that friends appreciate and thrive on. There were often just quiet moments when they could sense the closeness and warmth of two people who are in sync. The love between friends has its own perfection, its own special nuances to reaffirm that each moment is special.

Bee looked deeply into her friend's brown eyes, "When do I get to read what you have finished so far?"

"I have not written enough to satisfy me, so it won't satisfy you."

"That's not true. I am not as hard on you as you are on yourself."

"That is a writer's lot. An artist's too, as I swoon over your paintings as does everyone else, and you declare it could be better. I think I'll have Bailey enjoy a romantic fling in the book," Cee offered after taking a sip of coffee.

"I'd much rather you have a romantic fling."

"It takes two to tango, dear heart. I can conjure up a playmate for Bailey, but when the well is dry even the dipper comes up empty."

"Maybe you need to get away from here for awhile, to take some trips to give yourself a better chance at finding your soul mate. Some lucky fellow is out there who will recognize you are Bailey and so much more."

Celia chuckled. "You should be the writer. You have a wilder imagination than I have."

"Once again you do not give yourself enough credit."

"It's not a question of credit. It is a matter of facing the real life for me, and accepting that opportunity has passed me by. I am not sad about it. My life, thanks to you, is full and satisfying."

"You know that is fatalistic and defeatist. It should never be too late to grab the gold ring. Some people do not find love until later in life, but that does not make it any less sweet."

" I do not foreclose anything, as no writer or person should. Yet, because of you and your family, also my family, I do not feel deprived."

"It is not the same thing. You have so much love to give, and there is room above and beyond what is here and now."

"It has to be," Celia sighed. "If I did not believe that I would be miserable. As it is, my happiness makes me productive and upbeat." She paused long enough to reach for and grasp Becca's hand firmly. "I do promise you that I will not close my book completely just yet. It is probably a good idea for me to get more exposure if only for the sake of my books, and I will recognize and pursue any reasonable opportunities. I have in mind going to more literary events."

Bee returned the pressure on Celia's hand. "Now you are talking!"

*Either write something worth reading or do
something worth writing.*

Benjamin Franklin

*The vision that you glorify in your mind,
the ideal that you enthrone in your heart –
this you will build your life by, and this
you will become.*

James Allen

FOUR

The workshop was held in a seminar room comprised of a long rectangular table with twenty chairs around it. Eight graduate students had signed up for the sessions, five females and three males.

Connor was sitting at one end of the table as the students staggered in. When he counted eight present, he began speaking in a low voice. "Welcome fellow writers!" He gazed from face to face, noticing that the students were older looking than the freshmen in the writing class. Would a degree of maturity prompt better writing and a more genuine interest in writing? "You are here to taste the passion and the pain of writing. I will guide you but not ease the way. Struggles are the lessons of life. Be prepared to agonize as the lessons become apparent. Since this is a small enough group, we can consider ourselves a family with no holds barred. Our first act will be to become acquainted, and to appreciate who we are. We'll go around the table and you tell us who you are, your writing experiences, and describe what you expect to get out of the workshop."

Connor took a deep breath. "I will start. My name is Connor Chase, and yes that is my real name and has not been changed. I have been writing since I was knee-high to a grasshopper. The early attempts were for my eyes only. I did not have the sense to stop even though the writings were not good, and maybe that was a good thing. Knowing nobody would read them was like a personal secret that made me look constantly within myself. I knew that I enjoyed writing, and I did it every chance I could get. Little snippets of the life of a boy in New York City, the frantic pace and diversity of people providing such a boy with eyes and ears wide-open to scribble observations and reactions. The writing boy stayed with me throughout the growing and grown years. As you know from the class syllabus, I have had four novels published, and many seem to enjoy them. This elixir and mystery of it all becomes apparent when I read and reread my own works. To my amazement, each time I find new meaning in what I wrote. I gain a great insight into who I was at the time and the hidden agenda for the person I wanted to become. I do not have the germ of a plot for book number five, I am somewhat impatient to begin the writing. Through you and what we do here, I am hoping an idea will develop and I will start the trial of my mind once again."

He nodded to the woman sitting to his left. She was petite with dark black eyes and long straight black hair. For an instant, an image of Dorie flashed before his eyes. "I am Leah Goldstein. I received my undergraduate degree in journalism, and I have dabbled in short fiction writing since high school. I find it comforting when I write, like visiting an old friend. It is pleasing myself without any concern for or about others. Hopefully, this workshop will give me a clearer understanding of me and the potential for any further writing."

Another young woman was next. She had short brown hair surrounded by a nearly perfect oval face with extremely clear complexion. She took off the brown-framed glasses before she spoke, her diction was as clear as the complexion. The words were delivered with a tinge of an accent. "My name is Bernadette La Rouche, and obviously I am French. I have done some writing now and then and not sure if I really ever enjoyed it. It is frustrating to want to say something profound and the words come slowly, if at all. Yet, it holds a certain fascination for me. When I saw this workshop being offered, I figured it might be a good place for me to find out if I have a true writing desire and even any talent."

The man sitting next to Bernadette had a lean face, almost gaunt, matching a rather high-pitched voice. "My name is Ken Trollop. I wrote for the college newspaper for nearly my entire undergraduate studies. I have done some writing on my own recently, nothing I care to brag about. I am hoping all of this writing and the workshop will be a foundation for the book I would like to write on my family history, even if I need to fictionalize part of it. I have done genealogy research and there are interesting tidbits, not enough to fill a book but my relatives would be thrilled if I pursued it. I traced my family routes from a first settlement in Canada and gradual migration down along the St. Lawrence and Hudson Rivers."

The next person in order was a woman with long blonde hair. Her face was child-like, and at first glance one might think she belonged in Connor's freshman class rather than in a graduate workshop. "I am Gwen Jenner, and I was a drama student at Blantyre. You may have seen me in one of the school's theater productions. No leading roles, but the stage is in my blood. While I have not done any serious writing, I dream about staring in a play that I have written myself. I suppose I am here to take a step in that direction without falling on my face."

"Good planning," Connor enthused when the woman stopped. "After you have decided what you want to do, it certainly helps to know how to do it." The students laughed.

"I am Len Wheeler," the next student chimed in. His broad shoulders appeared to portray an athletic tilt rather than a writing endeavor. "A compulsive hobby of mine has been to write snippets of the antics people engage in to meet or escape from life. These range from philosophical to humorous. Some defy labeling. I guess I am here seeking a support bridge."

The last of the males spoke next, a man with a full beard. "I'm called Gordy although my full name is Gordon, Gordon Anterwick. Sounds like a strong pen name. but was a mouthful when I was growing up. I have written a bunch of things, mainly short stories and essays. I would like to become a political speechwriter or even a ghostwriter. I have taken numerous writing classes and frankly have not gotten much out of them. Too much emphasis on the technique. A workshop might prove more practical, and I am eager to throw myself into it if it promises to give back to me."

"Let's hope so," Connor exclaimed. "Any failure in that department will probably be mine and not yours."

After a brief pause, a young woman, tall and lanky, took up the gauntlet. "I am Gloria Feld. My mother, Florence Feld, is an author of more than a dozen romance novels. You may not recognize the name, but she has been quite successful in that genre. Surrounded by her special talent and accomplishments, I have been wondering whether I may have inherited her gift. She has never pushed me to write, but there have been some subtle suggestions bordering on that direction. The writing I have tried in her shadow has been strained and nothing I can shout about. It has not been enjoyable, but I do not think I should give up just yet. She has suggested I take a course in writing to help ease the way, so when I saw this offering I decided this will be my last hurrah, the last gasp. Either I will wind up following in her footsteps or a new path awaits me."

Connor fixed on the alluring hazel eyes. "Writing is difficult when done for yourself. When done for others it may be impossible. As on all avenues of life's journey, you need to be your own person. There is no lasting contentment if you live your life or write just because it is expected that way by someone else."

Gloria nodded in agreement. "I'll try to approach it that way."

"I am Vera Aldearn." The last student to speak was somewhat older than the others with unruly hair and overweight. "As is obvious, I had put off my college education until later in life. I have had considerable work experience, trying many fields without any to my liking. Many involved business writing, but I think my calling is in the world of fiction. I have a book idea dying to break loose, a fictionalized compilation of family anecdotes to amaze and amuse. The idea arises from the fact that I have a family unlike so many others. I have studied writing and I feel this workshop can get me going."

Connor nodded. "Well, you are certainly an interesting bunch of folks. I think we will have a good and productive time here. Yet, with so many other facets of life, the more effort you put into it the more you are going to get out of it. We'll put the theory into practice that the more you write the easier it will become. We'll see.... rather, we'll write. For starters, for next week write a short story, one or two pages double-spaced in length. Handle this scenario...... You are a stranger in a small town. How did you get there? What do you do? Give special thought and emphasis to the opening and closing sentences. Make sure you give it a title. It is, writing doctor, your baby to deliver."

The secret of good writing is to say old things
in a new way or to say new things in an old way.

Richard Harding Davis

If you don't like something change it; if you
can't change it, change the way you think
about it.

Mary Engelbreit

Sometimes it's the smallest decisions that
can change your life forever.

Keri Russell

FIVE

Four students dropped out of the writing class. Connor hoped those remaining would have taken his preliminary warning and overview seriously and throw themselves earnestly into the readings and exercises. The rewards could be plentiful and might very well extend beyond writing. Expressing oneself clearly and forcefully fosters confidence and respect.

After taking the attendance, Connor asked for volunteers to read aloud the paragraph prepared on a personality trait. One woman raised her hand, the same one with straight brown hair and glasses that had spoken first at the last class session. He had concentrated on who responded when he took the attendance. "Abigail Torrance, is that right?"

"Yes," she smiled revealing the nearly universal perfect teeth of the younger generation.

"Please read your paragraph. When reading, stand or sit as you feel most comfortable doing."

She remained seated and cleared her throat. "At first blush, you would think my overly candid reaction to events and people is a weakness rather than a strength. Yet, it does enable me to be an observer and in analysis of those things brought to the surface. I do not let things get bottled up inside for worry and frustration as there is no chance for them to fester."

"And are you especially candid about apologizing and admitting you are wrong if your reaction is off the mark?"

"Oh, yes," she smiled again. "That is also a component part of being candid. I am even candid enough to admit that I am wrong more often than I am right."

"What if you offend or hurt others?"

"That is their problem, not mine."

"How can that be if you are the prime mover? I concede that a certain degree of candidness can be a positive, but it should be tempered with consideration not to mention that you have all of your ducks in a row."

Her reply was, naturally, forthright. "People should appreciate that I tell it like it is. What does it mean to have all my ducks in a row?"

"You are telling it not like it may really be but only as it appears to you. Having your ducks in a row means having all of the appropriate facts and in their proper sequence so that your conclusions are as justifiable as possible. Any one else frothing at the mouth to read their paragraph?"

A male with long sideburns, a vestige of a past era, raised his hand. Connor recognized him. "Ronnie DeWitt, is that right?"

"Yeah. And, my last name is most appropriate for my most powerful personality asset......a keen sense of humor. As I am a wit, for sure I am DeWitt. As I see older generations struggle to maintain an economic and social life that they deem so necessary, life takes on too serious a role, too many adverse connotations. Better to laugh and shrug it off. Poking fun at people is enchanting entertainment. Making people laugh or at least to crack a smile is most satisfying."

"What if the last joke is on you? When you graduate and seek a place in the work force and you are confronted by the economic and societal demands that go with it, you may find it no laughing matter."

"The way I figure it, once I can't or shouldn't laugh at others, I can always laugh at myself."

"I do hope it works out for you that way." Connor looked around the room as another male raised his hand. "John Yodder?"

"That's right."

"Fire away."

"I am trying out to participate in the next winter Olympics as a member of the United States cheapskate team. The polite word is frugal, but I am just downright cheap and proud of it. I've reduced it to a science to save money whenever any expenditure is involved. I'd walk a mile out of the way to save a few cents. I won't even date a girl unless she pays her own way." He hesitated for the boos from the females in the room. "It is a given, an adventure, and it is who I am."

"A definitely unpopular personality trait when it affects others. I suppose if a girl offered to pay for you, you would marry her." Laughter filled the room.

"Especially if her family were wealthy." More laughter arose.

"If that comes to pass, see if she has a sister for me." Again, laughter was raucous. "That was a light-hearted paragraph and entertaining for a reader. Certainly, such can be a lofty and satisfying goal for a writer. Well done, Mr. Yodder."

Next to raise a hand was a woman wearing a bright yellow sweater with a matching ribbon tying back long brown hair. "Deborah Barnes, right?"

"Sure enough." She stood up and looked around before reading aloud the words on the paper she was holding in a firm grip. "I have a personality trait that most would not know about, at least at first. Yet, it is very important to me. I am an extremely patient person with people and situations. It is almost as if I am waiting for the final event in a protracted series to take place. I do not prejudge people and do not jump to conclusions. I hope I am this way all of my life, especially when I become a parent. I have seen first-hand what impatience can do to a child, especially the withering away of confidence and self-esteem. I was particularly taken when you mentioned at our last class that a writer needs patience. At least I have that quality. Talent may be another matter."

"Patience is a sound foundation to build on for many other facets of life and living. How did you develop such a worthwhile feature?"

"I'm not sure. It just seemed to be a natural way to greet each event and person. It was as if I kept telling myself to look, listen, and learn."

"Has it ever worked to your disadvantage?"

"Sure, but on the whole I just know it makes me a better person."

"Well, more power to you, young lady. I liked the way you led into the topic. The lesson here is you do not want to insult the intelligence of the reader. Everything does not have to be spelled out and every conclusion stated. Often it is best if the reader fills in some of the obvious gaps and reaches the kind of conclusion the writing is directed at. Later on, if you confirm what the person has thought, they will feel better and you can sit back satisfied that your writing has done its job."

He asked the students to pass their writings to the front. Once collected, he continued, "I am leaving it to your own devices to keep current with the readings. There will be an unannounced written quiz on occasion as well as ongoing discussions. It would be best for all if each of you can make contributions to such a dialogue. For the next session, please write a one-page description of what you would do if you wrote a novel, it has been published, and it has become a best seller. Don't ever be afraid to dream. Concentrate on an attention getting first sentence. Give it a catchy title."

A few students lingered after the others had left asking him questions and engaging him in conversation. That pleased him. Perhaps, his message was getting across to them.

Writing, at its best, is a lonely life.

Ernest Hemingway

He is outside everything, and alien everywhere.
He is an aesthetic solitary. His beautiful,
light imagination is the wing that on the
autumn evening brushes the dusky window.

Henry James, referring to
a writer

*Too many people miss the silver lining
because they're expecting gold.*

Maurice Setter

SIX

It was a picture-perfect autumn day and Celia was going to take full advantage of it. After writing a couple of paragraphs in Ghost of the Mountain she put the leash on Sherlock and they walked leisurely to Bee's gallery. A wonderful part of living in a small town is that nearly everything is within walking distance. She would then pick up a few things at Frank's store before returning home.

Rearranging the paintings on the wall, Becca glanced out the large storefront window and saw Cee and Sherlock approaching. "I wish so hard that I could arrange her life as easily as I do these paintings," she thought to herself. As much as her painting was fulfilling for her, it was the marriage and children that gave the basic substance to a rewarding life. She wanted that so much for her dear friend. Wishing was not enough, and it was evident all that she could do in the absence of finding someone for her was to encourage and support the person in this world that was special to her. She greeted Cee light-heartedly. "You must have had a thought gem to add to our morning conversation."

"I just wanted to give you another hug. You mean so much to me." The women hugged closely. "That certainly was worth walking to."

"I sold a painting this morning. That's why I am moving some around. An elderly couple from Charlotte who had been in before came back and bought the snowscape with the red barn."

"Ah, that is a wonderful painting, as they all are. I am sure they will love it."

"They were tickled with it. I made sure they took one of your brochures and invited them to browse through your books on the shelf, but they were totally absorbed in the painting."

"Probably a good thing. I'd have to pay you a commission if they bought a book,"

"I already had my hug. That's all the compensation I need. How does the arrangement look?"

"Fine. There is no way they could look bad unless you flipped them over and just showed the backside."

"I never thought of that. Perhaps I should paint a picture on the reverse side as well and sell them two for the price of one."

"That idea should be worth another hug." They hugged warmly. There is great comfort in a hug earnestly meant and generously offered.

"There is no way you could write a bad book."

"That surely is an unbiased opinion."

"Being President of your fan club carries with it great responsibility."

"You'll be further proud of me. I signed up to do a presentation at the North Carolina Writer's Organization book fair next month in Greensboro. They are having a special panel for already published authors."

Bee grinned. "Good for you, Bailey."

"I'll be gone for three days. You'll have to take care of this fur ball."

"It will be a strain but somehow I can manage."

"I might come back married."

"Better still."

"Wouldn't that shock you?"

"Perhaps, but also please me at the same time. Not all shocks are bad."

"You know I really don't hold out any prospects for finding a fella. But, it would be nice to be among other writers and hear some inside stories and secrets."

"Please do not foreclose anything. Wear a short skirt and a tight top that shows some cleavage. Smile often and laugh at all of the bad jokes. Pretend you are Bailey at her wildest if you have to."

"You want me to meet someone under false pretenses?"

"If it works, why not? Once he bites, the rest is history."

"Because there is me and then there is Bailey. If it is not the real me he wants then even Bailey would balk."

"Ah, but he would get both. You are Bailey if only between the pages."

"But not between the bed sheets."

"All the more wondrous."

They hugged once more. Bee watched as Cee picked Sherlock up in her arms and headed to Frank's store. Bee said softly to herself, "Yes, that woman has so much love to give."

Celia joked with Frank and then started towards home with a bag of necessities and Sherlock in tow. Once again she was amazed at her good fortune having Bee as a life-long friend and her warm support for all of her endeavors. She felt sorry for anyone who does not have such a close friend. It is more precious than gold to have a person who understands your needs, can cushion the disappointments, and help celebrate the successes. One who does not sit in judgment. One who is there in any helpful capacity.

After a satisfying lunch of cottage cheese with peaches, Cee luxuriated in the calmness of the day and the warmness of her thoughts. She supposed she was not as happy as she could be. After all, happiness is a never-ending quest. Yet, she was content with her life and satisfied in who she was. Growing up she had no unusual dreams of success in any chosen pathway. All that she wanted was to be a good person and to share in a special love. Writing was a hobby not an all or nothing venture. While love with a man might be ideal and, secretly, she had believed that long before this she would have found that kind of love, it did not consume her time or thoughts. She had the love of friendship and family and that smoothed out the bumps in the road and added to the scenic byway. She echoed Bailey's magical creed expressed in all of the books – "If you don't have great expectations you don't have big disappointments."

We do not write in order to be understood;
we write in order to understand.

Cecil Day Lewis

The two most engaging powers of a good
author are to make new things familiar
and familiar things new.

William M. Thackerry

Nobody can go back and start a new beginning,
but anyone can start today and make a new
ending.

Maria Robinson

***

SEVEN

Faculty housing consisted of a series of two-story townhouses several blocks from the University. Except for the end units, each had a common wall with the two adjoining units. The main level had a living room, bathroom, and an eat-in kitchen. The second level had two bedrooms and a bathroom. Families requiring more space had to rent a house in the town or beyond. Two parking places were in the front. It was an easy walk to the campus unless one had to go to the School of Law or several other academic buildings that were on the far end of the grounds.

Connor's scant furniture and possessions that had filled the studio apartment in the city were easily spread out in the townhouse. He planned to use the second bedroom as a writing den. He placed his desk beneath the window that had a nice view beyond the houses in the valley to the majestic mountains in the distance.

He spent Saturday finishing setting up the kitchen, doing laundry in the stacked machines in a closet off the kitchen, and then vacuuming the entire place. A trip to the grocery to stock up finished the day.

It was during an early morning walk on Sunday with a cool misty rain falling and making his face damp that the idea came for the new novel. Why not write a story about writing? He could use a Professor of Creative Writing as the protagonist and employ the actual interplay with the current students as the force of the stress and rewards of writing. There might be a more limited readership for such a topic, but it certainly would be relevant and engrossing for him to write. Too bad the perfect book title was already taken on an older classic – *The Agony and the Ecstasy*.

Just as his mind took flight on imaginary wings, he noticed a figure just ahead walking a small dog. The woman was wearing a raincoat with the collar turned up and a wide-brimmed rain hat pulled snuggly down over her head. The dog had a slicker on and seemed impervious to the wetness.

The pair turned in to the unit four doors down from his. As they did, the woman turned to him and smiled. "Only a restless professor would be out and about early on a day such as this." Her voice was soft and mellow.

He returned her smile. "You have me pegged right. A restless spirit combined with a cramped body and a boundless mind."

"Sounds serious. I hope it is not contagious. I guess you are a neighbor as well."

"Right again. I'm four units further down. I am Connor Chase, English Department."

She smiled again, a warm and inviting smile. "And I am Kelly Hagger, Sociology Department. This is my faithful companion Gil, short for Gildersleeve, a mixed terrier I got at the pound last year and we are inseparable. How long have you been teaching here?"

"I just started. And you?"

"This is my third year. In a way it seems like just yesterday but I am in my element, although this weather is certainly not part of that element. It is one miserable day. Would you like to come in for some coffee?"

"Sounds enticing, but besides needing to get fully settled in I have a bunch of papers to grade and other demanding tasks hanging over my head."

"Too bad. I made an apricot cake last night. I can offer you an extra large slice with the coffee."

"There goes my feeble resistance." He followed her into the house. All of the units had the same floor layout but revealed the decorative hand of the renter. Here the decorations were simple but in good taste. The mixture of colors matched just right, and there were attractive accents with mainly animal figurines placed around on the tables and shelves by the books. "Nice place. I could use your interior decorator."

"I doubt if you could afford my rates."

He took off his wet shoes at the door when he saw her do that. After she wiped the dog's paws with a towel and took off his slicker, she took off her raincoat and hat and placed them on a wall hook by the door. She was younger and more attractive than he had thought at first, and a form-fitting sweat suit showed an ample figure. There was a distinct sheen to the long brown hair. He put his raincoat on an adjoining hook and followed her into the kitchen.

He sat at the table watching her astutely preparing the coffee and cutting the cake. "Do you always bake a cake in the event you might meet a cold and hungry stranger?"

"I just had a feeling I would come across a tall, dark, and handsome stranger today."

"I hope I will do until he shows up."

"You fit the bill. I am not accustomed to having a stranger in the house, but there is a certain safe feeling in this faculty housing. Let's just say we are a breed apart. How can I not trust an English Professor? I like to bake. It is a family tradition. Of course, eating the product forces me to exercise or I'd be a blimp. What do you take in your coffee?"

"Just black, please."

"That's the way I like it. No extra calories to compete with the cake."

"I am trying to place your accent."

"Upstate New York, Syracuse to be exact. Without a doubt you are a New

York City boy. There is no mistaking that."

"Guilty as charged."

"Scary if you ask me. I visited there once. Everyone was rushing somewhere or nowhere. I couldn't tell the difference."

"Adapting is the key. If you can't fight 'em, join 'em." She started to gather up the coffee cups and cake plates to bring them to the table. "May I help you?"

"You can help by eating all of the cake. I'm extremely sensitive about my baking capabilities."

"Shouldn't be a hardship." One bite confirmed that conclusion. "Best cake I've had in a long time, if ever. So, what do you teach?"

Her smile was tantalizing and voice mesmerizing. "I teach Family Relationships and General Sociology 101. I wrote a text on families as a unit when I was in graduate school that somehow caught the attention of the academic world and this teaching opportunity opened up. It is my calling, I guess, because I love it."

"Do you have a family of your own?"

"No husband or children. I am the oldest of seven children, so you might say I know families inside and out. And what is your forte?"

"I am teaching a freshman class in Creative Writing and a graduate workshop. I have written four novels."

"Wow! I am in the midst of a celebrity. Sorry I never heard of you. What are your books about?"

"I like to think they are thoughtful stories examining the vital lessons of life. You can look my name up and it will lead you to my website. There you can find out more about them than you probably ever want to know. Actually, while walking this morning I had an idea for my next book. It is about two strangers who meet in the rain."

"Didn't you know there is no such thing as a stranger? There are just friends you haven't met yet."

"Seriously, though, just before I met you I did have a rare brainstorm. I was hoping the benefits of teaching here would be to get an idea for the next book and then the time to work on it."

"They say apricot cake congeals thoughts."

"I believe that. I thought I would write a story about writing. I can use the classroom actions to add to what I already know and believe. I am on panels or a guest speaker at book-sponsored events. Maybe the theme can light a fire and inspire."

"Sounds like a book title right there as well as a worthy undertaking writer man. I have been collecting notes over the past year to start a new text on the projected family of the future. Maybe, we can rename this housing complex Writers Row."

They spent the next hour in concentrated conversation. He had two pieces of cake and three cups of coffee. She wrapped up an extra piece for him to take home. They exchanged telephone numbers and she hugged him before he went through the door. It was a warm and endearing gesture. He imagined there are many unrestrained affectionate mannerisms in larger families. He did not want to jump ahead of himself, but this promised to be a meaningful friendship, if not more.

Kelly stared at the closed door for a moment. She had taken an instant liking to Connor and hoped the feeling was mutual. It was a bold action to invite him into her home, someone she had not met before. Instinctively, she had a safe sense about him. Being a sociologist, she hoped she was a good judge of character. Being a woman, she hoped she could predict a possible relationship. As the oldest in the family, there had always been some demanding features within the home that infringed on social involvements. As the oldest, she was probably the only one assured of going to college, although the others of age that followed her all had made it so far. In college she tried to make up for earlier social deprivations. She even went steady for a year, a combination that deteriorated as her interests centered on intellectual involvement and he became more sports minded. At Blantyre, she had not met anyone who raised her interest until now. The academic surroundings had been a challenge and she was enjoying teaching. Her twenty-seventh birthday was in two weeks. She liked to think that Connor was an early birthday present.

Back at his house, Connor took off his shoes at the door believing this would be a good habit to get into. He put the cake on the kitchen counter and headed up to the writing den. Opening the laptop, he typed in the first paragraph of the now inspired book.

Every person's story is a page from life. A novelist collects and arranges those pages using imagination as the transport for the hopeful journey to a satisfying and thoughtful destination, a poignant passage. Events and characters, imaginary or to some degree real, are threaded throughout to help produce the profound, tickle the fancy or lead thoughts and feelings to places memorable and significant. Ongoing deliberations and numerous rewrites set a true and definite course for the excursion.

He closed the laptop and started reading the student papers. He stopped after a short time and gazed out the window. A warm lingering thought spread in his mind just as the fog shrouded the mountains in the distance. Perhaps this was the day for a bunch of new beginnings.

Daniel Hill Zafren

*Everyone walks past a thousand story ideas every day.
The good writers are the ones who see five or six of
them.   Most people don't see any.*

Orson Scott Card

*The imagination of fiction writing is always hard to
describe to nonwriters, those tunnels in the unconscious,
those flitting responses to what might have been, what
possibly could be.*

Carol Shields

*Don't judge each day by the harvest you reap but by
the seeds that you plant.*

Robert Louis Stevenson

***

EIGHT

When the freshmen class was seated and the attendance taken, Connor looked intently at each person. Assured that firm eye contact was made, he spoke slowly and emphatically. "Before we get to the assignment for today, I want to read one of the paragraphs submitted last week." He picked up the sheet of paper from the pile on the desk.

Looking in the mirror, I asked myself "What is my strongest personality trait? Do I even have a personality?" Everyone has a personality. They come in all shapes and sizes. It is far easier to describe or even analyze a personality of others, even being able to fix on what is the strongest or most favorable component assuming you know them well enough. I am puzzled looking at myself. I do not have a strongest trait. Then it dawned on me. My strongest trait is that I do not have a strongest trait. Each facet of my personality is fully developed and totally exercisable. I am for the lack of a better term, well rounded.

Connor sat on the edge of the desk. "What do you think of this piece?"

Claude Evans in the front spoke out. "I liked it. It was incisive, interesting, and well-written."

"Of course, you would. It is your masterpiece." The class laughed. "I do agree with you. It captured my attention. Have you done writing before?"

"A little. I'm not good at striking out on my own. If I am told what to write about, it seems to come easily."

"Well, you will probably like the next assignment. After that, we will see if you sink or swim on your own."

"Can I get my final grade now?" Again the class laughed.

"Do you really want an Incomplete?" More laughter. "Back to business. As a prelude to some of the outside readings due today to solidify the writing environment and backbone, who wants to describe the cynical approach offered about writing by William Zinsser? He was not surprised by the silence that shrouded the room. "Realizing that it takes some effort to do the readings, just remember you will be rewarded by having some interesting anecdotes to spout at parties and impress and entertain others, not to mention avoiding the embarrassment of handing in a blank paper if I give you a quiz on what certain writers think and portray about the writing process and life's mission. Well, he said, 'Clutter is the disease of American writing. We are a society strangling in unnecessary words, circular construction, pompous frills and meaningless jargon.' Would anyone care to read the masterpiece due today on feigned success?"

He anticipated that Abigail would be the first to volunteer following her earlier pattern of leading off. She took the bit and stood up quickly to read from her paper.

FIRST CLASS

*I am Abigail Torrance, author of the book now at the top of
the New York Times Best Seller List, "First in My Class."
I do try not to let fame and fortune dictate my behavior,
but it is wonderful having substantial royalties and all
sorts of attention bestowed on me. Of course, I will always
be me, the same one that described the rise by leaps and
bounds from mediocrity in a writing class to the one at the
head of the class. Despite some keen competition I emerged
with all of the plaudits, all of the awards. Hidden talent
unmasked. I was first in my class, establishing me as a
first class writer.*

*Sooner or later, and I do hope it is later, much later,
some other author's book will replace mine at the top of
the list. I intend to be gracious about it, if I can. After all,
nothing as fragile as a best-seller stays that way forever.
If the plan materializes, my new opus will be completed
by then and in contention for king of the road. So,
beware fellow travelers that I do not run you over once
more!"*

Connor smiled. "I suppose if I don't give you an A you will claim I am jealous and revengeful?"

"Makes perfect sense to me." The class broke out in loud laughter.

"I am sure it does." More chuckles from the throng. "I do admit you are the first to volunteer, and that is a good sign. I also like what you wrote, and it does show promise. Yet, first in the class is a bit too strong." Once again a wave of laughter. "Would anyone like to make claim to being second in the class? Don't be bashful." Deborah Barnes raised her hand. "Ah, Miss Patience, at least you waited for the second slot."

Deborah did not stand and read deliberately from her paper. She kept looking around the room as if to reassure herself that all were listening.

TO DO IT AGAIN

One might argue that after struggling for seven years to write a book that it is just and proper for it to rise to the golden heights. Even without heralded success, the initial reward was the completion of a spellbinding story with fascinating characters. I never tired of all of the rereads and rewrites. Freshness is its own allure and works its own magic. A good mother does not tire of her child. My book, throughout the seven-year gestation period was my baby. Now, others, many others, not only recognize the worth of the baby but also appreciate its fashionable outfits, its antics, and its unusual and substantial promise.

Amidst the clamor for me to write a sequel, for now I prefer just to bask in the spotlight. I am not sure I could face another extended period of frustration in trying to attain perfection. Yet, I know I will do that eventually. A writer must write and success is an elixir. It is like a nugget of chocolate. One bite does not satisfy. It only tempts the urge for more. So, excuse me if I do not rest on my laurels, do not use my newly acquired riches to retire. Rather, I retire to my library to begin another seven-year period. You might say that it is another form of the seven-year itch.

Connor nodded his approval. "Any comments?" Nobody spoke up. "Deborah, it was interesting. One pitfall authors fall into and need to be cautious about is in the guise of trying to be profound writing something that is a struggle for the reader to grasp and understand. For example, what does it mean, if I am repeating it correctly, when you say freshness is its own allure and works its own magic?"

"I was trying to say that if you say something new and exciting it captures the fancy of both the writer and the reader."

"Then why not add that to the description? It expands and clarifies so that the reader does not have to overly struggle to grasp what is meant. It is probably a fine line between making a statement that you want the reader to ponder over and fill in the full meaning and making the reader wonder what it is all about and question why the author did not explain it more completely. In this case, it might be more compelling to state: Freshness is its own allure and works its own magic because saying something new and exciting captures the fancy of the writer and the reader."

There were no further volunteers so he collected the assignment papers. The next assignment was announced – a one-page reaction to your book that publishers have rejected and even a close friend had trouble getting through it and candidly reacts in the negative.

When Connor returned home there was a telephone message from Kelly that she wanted to read his books but when she went to the university library all copies were checked out. She assumed his students were reading them for enjoyment and credit. She wondered if he had any copies that she might buy from him.

Instead of calling her back, he pulled out a copy of each book from the cartons in the closet and took them over to her. She answered his knock on the door wearing another sweat suit and her face flushed. "This is a pleasant surprise. I was just exercising. Please come in."

He offered her the books. "These are for you. I am pleased you want to read them but please do not feel you have to."

"Oh, I do want to. I am intrigued about what a tall, dark, and handsome stranger writes about. I think it will be a good way to get to know you better. How much do I owe you?"

"Nothing. They are a gift to my delightful stranger."

"You'll never get rich by giving the books away."

"Riches come in many forms. Let's just say they are in trade for that scrumptious apricot cake."

"Better than that. I'll consider them a birthday present. My birthday is Saturday."

"I just had mine two weeks ago, my thirtieth."

"That's a nice coincidence. This will be my twenty-seventh year battling with society."

"Society does not stand a chance. Unless you are already spoken for, let me take you out to dinner on Saturday to celebrate the occasion."

"That would be wonderful, birthday boy."

"I'll pick you up at seven."

"Fine."

She stared at the books after he left and clutched them to her chest in a feigned embrace. She was anxious to read the books and was excited about Saturday's date. It was the kind of excitement that spread warmth through her body that lodged firmly in her heart.

Later that evening when Kelly made her daily telephone call home to the family, with only her parents and one sister still living at home, she could hardly contain herself and blurted out about going to dinner with the man she had met on her walk. As expected, the news was received with joy at that end. As the oldest child, there was an unspoken expectation that she would be the first to marry and Kelly just knew that her parents, those caring and understanding people who nurtured the family in every aspect of their lives, would be so happy when a first grandchild came along. Perhaps, there was more resting on this potential relationship with Connor than she was entitled to hope for.

There is no how to it, no how do you write, no how do you live, how do you die. If there were, nothing would lie in the deep and very delicate chain of life. It is the doing that makes for continuance. It is not the knowing of how the doing is done.

William Saroyan

When we long for life without difficulties, remind us that oaks grow strong in contrary winds and diamonds are made under pressure.

Peter Marshall

***

NINE

Gordon Anterwick was the first to volunteer at the workshop to read aloud his story about being a stranger in a town. He stood back from the table and with a dramatic flare began his tale.

THE NOWHERE TOWN

There are dreams you never wake up from. This was one of those, bordering on a nightmare. My car broke down on the back road I had taken as a shortcut, and with no other traffic on the road and no cell phone service, I wound up walking three miles to a town called "Wilson's Creek." It was early afternoon, and not a single person or car could be seen on the one-block commercial span. It was not comforting to not see a gas station, indicating there was probably no mechanic around.

I noticed a diner and approached it. I could see no movement through the window and the door was locked. The general store next to it was dark inside and the door also locked. I glanced up the street not seeing any sign of life. There was not even a public phone booth. I resisted my urge to shout out for help, a distinct feeling of uneasiness taking hold. How long had it been since I had experienced fear? I walked to the end of the row of stores. There was no movement anywhere. Beyond was a vast expanse of desolate road and woods.

It was then that I spied the metal sign on a lamppost. "This town was erected in 1983 by Magna Pictures for the production of the horror film No Reason to Call. It has been left in tact in gratitude for the State's permission to use this land. It has been dedicated as a State Historical Site."

He remembered seeing the movie. The drivers of a series of automobile breakdowns had walked to the town for help. None of them were seen or heard from again.

The class applauded. Connor joined in. "That sure was an audience pleaser. How did you come up with the idea?"

"I'm not sure I came up with it or it came on its own. I started with the premise of the breakdown and the walk to town. I have always liked horror movies. I guess the sequence just fell into place."

"You also did well with the opening sentence, although it might be more apt to say that there are dreams that you seem never to wake up from rather than portraying it as an absolute concept. The ending was also good by leaving the reader to deduce what might happen next. Suspense is a crowd pleaser."

Gloria Feld raised her hand to read her story. "I can't top Gordy's effort, but you will see my story sure is different."

LOVE FOUND

It is an obvious fact that there is no connection between the heart and the brain. I had a mad crush on Brian for over a year although he never paid any attention to me. So, when he stopped me on the campus walkway and confessed a strong attraction and passion for me, I was completely blown away. He did not want people to talk, and he suggested we meet for a romantic fling that Saturday at the Hideaway Inn in the town of Springvale some thirty miles away.

I can't even remember the drive as I was in a rapt state. I waited in the lobby of the inn for four hours before it dawned on me that he was not going to show up. It was no doubt a college prank or a dare to the handsome fraternity hero to arrange a tryst with that unattractive and slovenly girl who all knew worshipped him.

She should have been deeply hurt, but she realized she was more hungry than angry. The inn keeper directed her to a small bistro on the other end of the small town. It was nearly deserted, not a good sign for a Saturday evening. When the

*waiter came out of the kitchen, she recognized him as Paul
Granger from her English class. He was all smiles and
hugged her before showing her to a table. This was his
home town and he came there every weekend to help at
the restaurant owned by his father.*

*Paul lit the candle on the table and it sparked a glow in
her heart. Since there were only a few customers, Paul
sat with her through much of the wonderful meal. They
talked endlessly, and after her third glass of wine she
announced she would get a room at the inn and wanted
him to spend the night with her. He readily agreed, stating
emphatically, "My father is also the innkeeper."*

The class applauded. Connor smiled. "Your mother would be proud of you. I am not a keen fan of romance stories as to my way of thinking, maybe an unjustified bias, there is a degree of disassociation from reality, but they do have a tremendous following. You did show some of the key elements, such as anticipation, rejection, and then redemption. There was also a good opening and closing. Well done, Gloria."

Gloria beamed as she sat down, a deep blush forming on her cheeks. She thought to herself, "Move over, mother, here I come."

Bernadette La Rouche was the next reader. She remained seated, her French accent infiltrating the presentation of her creation.

ONE ROAD TO PARADISE

*It was not her dream job, but there is an often quoted French
saying, perhaps universal by now, a job is a job is a job.
Driving the two hundred miles for the interview was a
chore, accompanied by the stress of applying and then
the actual interview which was difficult. So, instead of
driving back on the boring interstate highway, she
decided to take the old highway which was used before
the interstate was built. She should still make it back by
nightfall.*

*Passing large farms, herds of cows, and spans of thick
woods, she was beginning to relax from the ordeal. A*

road sign indicated that it was twelve miles to Paradise. She smiled thinking that if only it would be that easy. Anyway, it might be a good place to get a meal. She had been too nervous to eat earlier in the day.

Paradise had certainly seen better days. The construction of the interstate as well as a shopping mall not too far off probably was its downfall as with so many other small towns across the country. With her degree in urban planning, she had studied numerous cases of such decay, obvious by vacant and run-down stores. A pall was cast over the place and a visitor could not wait to escape. She wished she could infuse her youthful vitality and burgeoning ideas to bring Paradise back to its heavenly place.

The blinking neon sign of the diner caught her eye, and she pulled the car into one of the many empty places before it. A woman in a yellow uniform was behind the empty counter. The only other patron was an elderly lady in a booth sipping from a cup of coffee.

Due to time and space constrictions, what transpired next must be summarized. Peggy Andrews, the waitress as well as the diner owner, is delighted to have someone new to talk with, and talk she does. She told me everything about Paradise, and even introduced me to the mayor, Daisy Winfield, who was the lady in the booth. After some additional conversation, Daisy said the town could use some new ideas for revitalization, even radical ones. It was arranged for me to meet with her and the two town aldermen the next morning. Peggy put me up for the night at her place. The meeting went well, and I was hired as the town planner. Paradise would not be lost, after all.

Applause from the class greeted Bernadette's smile. Connor grinned. "You were doing just fine until the end. Readers should not be short-changed with a summary of the plot or events. As a writer you also owe it to yourself to do a full blown tale. That does not mean you have to spell out every detail or present dialogue in full. For example, you can refer to a conversation covering certain preliminaries before setting forth the dialogue that propels the plot or leads to a greater understanding of the character. If there are legitimate and demanding restrictions, such as a word count for a short story contest or a space limitation for a story to be printed in a magazine or journal, or a professor's arbitrary instructions to limit a story to no more than two pages, after completing the full narrative during a reread and rewrite you can cut it down by eliminating or abbreviating certain descriptions and scale down or drop some dialogue. It is during this kind of revisit that you can zero in on the true gist of the story. More often than not, the streamlining will produce more satisfaction on your part. I am not saying it is easy. Any exercise of judgment can be a grueling wrestling match with no clear victor. There is probably no writer, much to his or her chagrin, who has not had to drop a favorite phrase, a satisfying exposition, or some catchy dialogue for the flow of the story."

There were no other volunteers. He collected the papers before he spoke again. "I hope this assignment was enjoyable. There will be no workshop next week as I will be away at a book fair. You will have the luxury of two weeks to work on your next story. There will be no limitations on subject but make it a short, short story. Let your imagination soar in full flight. Again, concentrate on an attention-getting opening sentence and a rewarding final one. Remember the more you write does not necessarily mean a higher grade or lead to a more profound tale. An often-quoted saying from an unknown source says it well, "Inside every fat book is a thin book trying to get out." Another saying by Christian Nevell Bover says it a slightly different way, "A book should be luminous not voluminous."

To write what is worth publishing, to find honest people to publish it, and get sensible people to read it, are the great difficulties in being an author.

Charles Caleb Colton

The most valuable of all talents is that of never using two words when one will do.

Thomas Jefferson

***

TEN

The freshmen were an anxious lot. Many hands were raised when Connor sought a volunteer to read the assignment on a rejected book. He called on a young woman who had not volunteered before.

Blythe Proctor was barely five feet tall, just a wisp of a woman. Long bangs came down nearly to her thick glasses. She did not reflect a healthy image, but when she spoke her booming voice erased all doubt that here was an individual, her very own person. She stood straight and proud and began reading from a green colored sheet of paper.

TO WRITE A WRONG

"Fly in the face of opposition," Betty Prock's father told her when she ran for President of the high school senior class. She took that advice to heart, and by way of long and hard effort she won that election. Many years later when the book she had labored writing for six years was turned down by every publisher she approached and also criticized by her dearest friend, she fully intended to fly in the face of opposition.

The book was a vital part of her being. Maybe all books are not meant to be shared with others, at least not at first. The writing totally satisfied her and she was proud of the achievement. She had read it so many times she nearly knew it by heart. There was not a word in it she felt should be changed. Do you live your life for others or for yourself?

Taking repeated historical lessons from the master artists where once talent had been recognized and fame established, earlier works then discovered became valuable based on the ensconced notoriety, her strategy took form. She would continue to write books. As each became acclaimed achievements, as she genuinely expected,

*the then revelation of the earlier rejected work would be
brought into its rightful place of prominence. Victory,
even a belated one, will be just as sweet.*

Connor joined the class in applause. "Well done, Blythe. I am not sure the premise is too realistic as fame and fortune do not necessarily prompt further success, although it probably helps. Anyway, your heroine would have to find that out for herself. I liked what you wrote, and I think your classmates approved. I especially enjoyed the play on words in the title. It shows promise, young lady."

Henry Farrell volunteered next to recite his story. Short and on the plump side, his thinning hair was unruly as if that might add some substance to it. He stayed seated, the hand holding the sheet of paper trembling slightly.

ACCEPTING NONACCEPTANCE

*Doomed from the start. As an experienced and respected
journalist, he had expected the transition to writing a novel
to not only come easily but with fast rewards of its own. He
was wrong on both counts. The writing was an exercise in
frustration accompanied by great stress. There were long
periods when he was unable to write or even focus his
mind on the story he intended to complete. When he finally
finished it he gave it to his wife to read. She was not kind
in her reaction. She thought the plot was disjointed and
the characters not fully developed. The dialogue was
described as too predictable.*

*He should have just graciously acknowledged such an
honest critique and attempted to redo it. His pride and
vanity intruded. It was not until seven publishers rejected
the book that he finally accepted the reality that the book
was not of sufficient quality. Nobody wants to be a small
fish in a big pond. Yet, you have to be a small fish before
you become a big fish.*

Henry nodded at the polite applause. Connor delayed his reaction for a moment. "You certainly did follow the assignment, maybe too strictly. You write well and the technique is there, but the ingredient of yourself is lacking. Some points would have been more compelling if you branched out, perhaps giving an analogy or setting forth a dialogue with the wife displaying the sentiments of each. The use of conversation can be very effective in developing the personalities and thoughts of the characters. There is a wide disparity between setting forth facts and opinions and presenting a scene where expressions of imagination and emotions give the reader a greater degree of enjoyment and understanding. Do not be discouraged. All of you are here to learn the need and ways of those expressions. Here is the place for you to experiment with presentation over format. It is merely a situation of letting yourself go."

Catherine Weintraub volunteered next. Straight long brown hair cascaded down around an oval face with wide eyes, a small nose, and thin lips. She stood up, her story set forth on a large manila card held up by slim fingers.

A WAY OUT

*If you are not satisfied with yourself, how can you please
others? She knew the book was not good. She was
bored with the undertaking, tired of dedicating time
to it that might be spent doing more exciting things.
The more she tried to improve it, the more frustrating
it became. She was not even sure now why she
started it, although it was probably more of a stubborn
pride that she could do anything that she put her mind
to doing. Doing something and doing it well, as she now
discovered, can be two totally different achievements.
In fact, doing something and not not doing it well is in reality
a failure. That was evident by publisher rejection of
the manuscript and even her boyfriend's candid weak
expression of approval. She sensed he did not want to
hurt her feelings.*

*What to do about it? Three options were apparent.
First, she could scrap it and go to some new adventure.
This would be the easiest solution, although it would
nag at her not achieving fully what she set out to do.
Obscurity would be difficult to adjust to after dreaming
of fame. Second, she could redo it, perhaps salvaging
some parts which might congeal with a renewed effort.
Yet, she had already tired of doing this. It proved to be
boring and a monumental effort. Third, she could just*

put it aside for a year or two and then come back to it
with a renewed spirit and determination.

A fourth option emerged several days later. She was
wealthy enough to hire a ghost writer to redo it, and
she could add some personal touches. This would
not do. It would not really be her book. It had to be an
honest product.

Then, as if a bolt of lightning hit her, she knew what to
do. It would be done all over again, an entirely new
book. It would have this exciting premise. A rejected
novelist struggles with four options about what to do
with the book. It would be a struggle between the four
options. An option about options.

The class applauded again. Any encouragement for others is a form of encouragement for themselves. Connor was solicitous. "A nice effort, Cathy. I especially like that you dealt with the mind of the writer. That touches the entire content of this course. It can be pleasurable for the reader to know the thoughts of the characters and their reaction to them. It is a human quality, easy to identify with and easy to appreciate. We will only have one class next week as I am going to be on a panel of published authors away from here. In the one class we will have, be ready to answer questions on the outside readings. The week beyond, prepare a paragraph or two on advising your younger sibling to avoid hurting others emotionally. Employ a fresh first sentence and close with a powerful final sentence."

Writing is an adventure. To begin with, it is a toy
and an amusement. Then it becomes a mistress,
then it becomes a monster, then it becomes a
tyrant. The last phase is that just as you are about
to be reconnected to your servitude, you kill the
monster and fling him to the public.

Winston Churchill

Look upon adversity as an opportunity in disguise.

Chinese Proverb

***

ELEVEN

Kelly was dressed and ready for the Saturday dinner date when Connor rang the doorbell. A distinct excitement enhanced the glow on her cheeks. Overall, there was a calmness that came from a swelling feeling that she was comfortable with and about him. Her life's design seemed to be taking shape. A career in teaching was fulfilling, and now a man had entered the scene and she could see herself with him permanently.

After helping her into the car and as they started towards the restaurant, she spoke slowly. "I finished your first book and have started the second one."

"Well, enchanting lady, what is your reaction?"

"I'll give you ten minutes to stop talking like that."

He chuckled. "Ten minutes of compliments for one who deserves them is merely a grain of sand on the beach of time. You can be candid. I am not sensitive about my writings."

"I liked the book very much. Perhaps, it is a bit too intellectual for the average reader. I felt close to the characters, and it did convey a powerful message."

"I strongly believe that all lessons in life are truly significant."

"I echo that for sure. Life is fragile and far too short to live it unwisely. I am frank to admit that in my earlier years because of a basic immaturity I was shaken by a series of misjudgments."

"Don't be too hard on yourself. I dare say there is no one who has been free of mistakes and has no regrets. The secret is to make sense of the mishaps, be stronger because of them, and to try and avoid future pitfalls."

"Easier said than done, professor."

"Ah, yes, a writer sure can pontificate."

The Italian restaurant was charming and the food quite good. They both had veal marsala with a side of spaghetti. The conversation was relaxed and easy.

At her door he took her in his arms. "I'm glad we both had the garlic bread." The kiss was tender and lasting. As he gazed into the hazel eyes, he sensed she was a special woman, perhaps just the woman he needed at this stage of his life. Thoughts of Dorie seeped into his mind, and he wondered if he could ever feel that same way about another woman. Kelly was intelligent, interesting, and a warm person. The prime attributes that were important to him. It was tempting to be close to her. All books are open until they need to be closed. Each page of life has and should have its own particular appeal and significance.

The kiss lingered on Kelly's lips. She was tempted to invite him in, hoping they would wind up in bed. It had been far too long since she was loved and loved in return. She fought off the temptation as she wanted to savor the budding relationship and to be content with each stage as a building block for a permanent relationship. If it were meant to be, everything would come in time.

Kelly's parents as well as brothers and sisters had called her earlier in the day to wish her a happy birthday. Since it was not late, she called the folks knowing they would be anxious to hear about the date. Even relating the events was as memorable as living them. She said it aloud before the thought fully took hold.......she was in love.

Later, as she lay in bed fully awake, her body and mind tingling with the amorous prospects so near, she recalled her first kiss when she was nine years old. It was utter chaos that day at the roller skating rink with three birthday parties overlapping. She was skating with her sister, Vera, when a wild bunch of boys smashed into them and sent them tumbling to the floor. One of the boys, Eddie Crowell, from the same home room class at school extended his hand to help her up. Just as she was fully erect, he kissed her firmly on the lips. She was too stunned to say anything or react, and he skated away with a big grin on his face. She castigated him the next school day, and he never tried that again. Secretly, she wished he had. She liked him and actually enjoyed that kiss even if not prepared for it.

When in junior high school, Buck Torren invited her to a party. It turned out to be a kissing party. All the couples sat around the room. The lights were turned out. A designated person sat on the floor in the middle of the room with a flashlight. When the light was shone on a couple they had to kiss for as long as the light was on them. During the dark periods, Buck kept putting his hand under her sweater to feel her breasts. At another party with him she had her first sexual experience. He coaxed her into a bedroom of the house and forced himself on her. It was quick and painful, and she was not even sure exactly how and why it happened. However, the mystery of it all that she had so many times discussed with her friends was not an enigma any more but just a fuzzy afterthought. Her understanding and loving mother later discovered the blood-stained panties in the hamper and then sat her down and talked to her at length about the difference between a lasting and meaningful physical relationship and a sexual experience based on the temptation of the moment. The family was always her safe haven and instilled in her those values now so precious. Her career was centered on that, and she was confident it would be the strong pillar to support the love leading to marriage and the family of her own.

Still looking back, there was the wasted year with Bert Smathers in college. The year they went steady was a roller coaster ride. There were times of elation, as well as a close and energetic physical relationship. There were many other periods of empty or forced conversation, as well as a grappling to find activities they were both interested in. He dragged her to football and basketball games, and she did not enjoy them. His attention to sports kept increasing and while she tried to be upbeat she just could not match his enthusiasm and had trouble concentrating on and understanding such activities. It was as if she had thrown that year on the garbage heap. Giving such prolonged concentration to a relationship that had little promise was disturbing and left her lonely and frustrated.

Sleep overtook her entity, and she hoped the bounty of all of her beautiful dreams would be fully realized. Total happiness was so close she could almost reach out and touch it.

An author is often obscure to the reader because they proceed from the thought to expression than like the reader from the expression to the thought.

Sebastian Roch Nicholas De Chamfort

I'm writing a book. I've got the page numbers done.

Stephen Wright

Live with your whole being all the days of your life. Your reward will be true happiness.

Rebecca Thomas Shane

***

TWELVE

Before the book conference, Connor spent two days visiting with his parents at the retirement home near Greensboro. Their health and attitude were good. It was a far cry from New York City but they liked it there and had made some new friends. Their minds were also sound, and there were many detailed talks as they reminisced about earlier days. Once the stories were flagged the memories were unfurled to the accompaniment of laughter and some tears. There can be distinct comfort in looking back in life. Savoring the moments about feats accomplished and plans fulfilled can be most enjoyable. To relive happy times with loved ones is highly rewarding. He felt good about them as he left for the conference.

Cee had already made the drive to Greensboro and checked in at the hotel where the conference was to be held for the next three days. The panel she was to be on was on the first morning. Various programs were scheduled at other times. Luncheons were provided at the hotel for attendees and the hotel had a continental breakfast for guests. Dinner and evenings were at individual discretion.

She had second thoughts about being there. Her comfort zone was at home and being close to Bee. The grounds surrounding the hotel had well maintained pathways, and she walked through them admiring the late blooming flowers and the fall foliage. She would make the best of being here. Bailey would not bat an eyelash in this situation.

Back in her room, she went over the notes she had prepared for the speech she would give the following morning. Each speaker was to make a presentation for five minutes and then the audience would be invited to offer comments or ask questions. Before going to the hotel's restaurant for dinner, she telephoned Bee. Bee assured her that Sherlock was well and further encouraged Cee to be on the lookout for romantic opportunities. Cee remarked that Bailey was on retainer for the conference and on the job scouting out the situation. Little did she know that chance was soon on hand and that there was no forewarning by Bailey.

At the panel table, she was placed next to Connor Chase. She had never heard of him, and he was already seated and going through his notes. He was more dignified than handsome, but his curly brown hair and bushy eyebrows sure did catch her attention. As she pulled out the chair he looked up at her and a warm smile infiltrated to her heart. His wide brown eyes were riveting, and it was an awkward moment before her forwardness took hold. "Thanks for saving the seat."

He liked what she said almost as much as he liked the full voice. She was not an attractive woman, and in her petite frame he noticed a slight stoop of the shoulders and back, perhaps a vestige from a childhood disease or deformity. "I would like to be your hero and let you believe I saved the seat, but frankly no one has yet been able to afford the seat fee."

"Ah, alas, you must surmise that I am an author and therefore poor. I have only words as my riches, so please take pity on me and let me rest where I can."

"Sounds fair. You can pay me in conversation."

"Not a problem." She sat down and could not help but notice his strong hands. Even Bailey would have been smitten.

Connor was struck by the freshness that Celia exuded. They introduced themselves, and he stared into the blue eyes beneath the blonde bangs. The short-cropped hair framed an oval face with a hint of freckles on the cheeks. He thought her to be quite young, and it was not until later that he found out she was nine years older than him.

Of the six authors on the panel, Celia's presentation was by far the most interesting and prompted the majority of comments and questions from the audience. Several people had read one or more of her books. Her presentation revolved around her heroine, Bailey Farrel, and the challenges in writing stories involving a continuous central figure whose alter ego slips into and becomes the author herself. A young woman in the audience who joyfully proclaimed she had read all of Celia's books, asked her if she could give a little preview of the next book.

Celia beamed. "Thank you, and I certainly count you now as one of my good friends. There is nothing an author likes better than talking about the writings that consume a vast amount of time and energy. The new book, still developing but a sizable chunk completed, may be Bailey Farrel's greatest challenge. It is entitled *The Ghost of the Mountain*. Don't let the title mislead you. There are no ghoulish figures or other paranormal features in the story. Rather, it is about the personal ghosts that haunt our lives. Amy Tan, a rather well known author, states it this way: 'Family ghosts hoard secrets that bewitch the living.' Bailey must confront things she cannot see."

At the end of the session, Connor turned to her. "Remind me never to be on a panel again on which you are a speaker. You lit up the audience and stole the limelight."

"Sorry."

"Don't be. It was wonderful watching and listening to you. You established an easy rapport with everybody in the room. Your presentation was relaxed and informative. I should take a lesson from you."

She smiled. "That is one great compliment, sir. You should know that if I was asked to do an encore, I would be mute. This was all there was."

"Modest, too. I think this was just the tip of the iceberg. You are a one person show."

"No. I am, if anything, a two-woman show. Bailey Farrel is so much a part of me there are times I am not sure if I am me or her."

"Well, then, will both of you join me for lunch?"

There was a distinct rustling in her heart. "It is fine for me, but I'll have to check with her. I think she will agree so long as you don't ask her too many questions. She confided in me that she is here to relax."

"That won't be easy as I am curious to know her better. I'll concentrate on you."

"Agreed."

"I will meet you at the doorway to Ballroom A where the lunch is being served."

"I'll be there. I mean we'll be there."

There was just enough time for Celia to go back to her room to freshen up. On the way, she pulled out her cell phone and pushed Bee's programmed number. Bee answered in her typical fashion. "This better be good,"

Cee was a bit surprised by the excitement in her own voice. "It is gooder than good." She could tell that Bee was speechless. "His name is Connor Chase, and I think he likes me better than Bailey. The three of us are going to lunch, and Bailey promised me that she will not speak at all. Got to run now, dear friend. More later."

Becca still had not hung up even though she knew Cee was no longer on the other end. "Oh, my gosh!"

Other than some polite conversation with the other people at the luncheon table, Connor and Celia talked in a steady stream. Their books, writing styles, and literary visions were quite different. Yet, experiences and soul wrenching devises were so similar that the animated discussion was reflective of that commonality and was fresh and comfortable. Other than with Bee, Celia could not recall being this frank and energetic in conversation. Connor soaked in all of Celia's open and gushing thoughts. It was so reminiscent of times with Dorie, moments as if there were windows to peer through to the heart and mind.

After lunch, they walked together through the grounds of the hotel. Connor reached for her hand and their fingers intertwined. The talk covered many areas of their backgrounds and dreams, including tantalizing interpretations of theories they had developed on their own as well as those asserted by others. Through it all was a closeness, a riveting aura that reflects an imponderable that things that should be strange are actually familiar. Being together for a few hours produced a timeless adhesion.

They attended two of the afternoon programs and then returned to their rooms. It was decided they would go to a restaurant a few blocks from the hotel for dinner. It would be an easy walk.

As soon as she closed the door, Cee telephoned Bee. Before Bee could say anything, Cee blurted out, "Do you believe in magic?"

Becca responded after a short pause, "I believe in you and that is all the magic I need. Tell me everything."

"I'm spending the best day of my life and it is not yet over." She related in detail the events that had occurred.

"Wow," was Bee's high-pitched reaction.

"We are going to dinner, and then find a Justice of the Peace." She laughed at her own joke. "I had to add a note of fiction just so you would know this is really me. Seriously, my cherished friend, this is the love of my life. I feel it in every inch of my body. Even Bailey has given me her blessings."

"You have mine as well, dearest, dearest friend."

"I'll call you tomorrow."

"I'll be waiting." After hanging up, Becca added, "Please make the magic real. Don't let her be hurt."

They borrowed a large golf umbrella from the hotel for the walk to the restaurant as a light rain was falling. It gave her an extra reason to hold firmly on to Connor's arm. The restaurant was quaint and quiet, and the table they had was in a separate alcove. The food was good, although secondary to the scintillating conversation as they further explored their minds.

It was raining hard when they left the restaurant. Connor felt the pressure on his arm from Celia's fingers and it was reassuring. Hearing the rain on the umbrella brought back the memory of camp and the first kiss with Marilyn Comstack. He stopped and turned towards Celia kissing her gently. A second kiss lasted longer and was tinged with fervor. It was a confirmation of a special feeling. Celia clutched his arm with added ardor.

At the door to her room they kissed several times, each a meaningful moment in their personal world of literature. She whispered in his ear, "Will you think less of me if I invite you to spend the night with me?"

"Nothing would please me more if you are sure that is what you want."

"I am a thirty-nine year old virgin. I have been waiting for the right man and the right moment. This is my dream turning into my reality."

They kissed again. His voice was barely audible. "Two rights cannot make a wrong."

"Bailey, the woman of the world, wants you as well."

"She'll have to find someone else. I only wish to be with you."

*Fiction is a glimpse of our common humanity, a
reminder of it, a generous engagement between
the reader and the imagined world of a book.
So much of what we do as writers, no matter how
grounded in the particular story it might be, is a
leap of faith.*

Susan Richards Shreve

*Cultivate caring and generosity. Happiness is
the natural state of a loving heart.*

Anonymous

***

THIRTEEN

As Celia drove home from the conference, Connor's kiss was fresh on her lips. In her novelist mind, that portrayed sensation was to last as long as the heart would hold on to it. For several days she had experienced an exhilaration that brightened her world to illuminate possibilities she had feared were far from her grasp. She could hardly wait to share all of this with Bee.

Connor had a late start, and he knew he would not be able to make the trip all in one day. He telephoned the Department's secretary to cancel his Tuesday class. He was looking forward to the drive to sort out his thoughts and feelings. For sure, he had never met a woman like Celia. It mattered not that she was older. He dared to believe that a woman with her vibrancy would always be youthful. It mattered not that others might call her homely or otherwise unattractive. To the perceptive eye the inner beauty was there to hold and revere. For a woman inexperienced in displaying passion, he had not ever felt the strength of love she showed except perhaps as his memory enhanced early times with Dorie. The drive and return to student involvement would help the dust to settle and enable him to gain a true picture of these emotional developments.

Cee drove directly to Bee's studio where she would be waiting with Sherlock. The hug was warm and held for nearly a minute. Cee clutched Sherlock close to her chest, feeling the waging tail thump against her body. "If it is a dream, please don't wake me up."

Bee stroked Cee's arm. "Tell me all you can. I don't want to wait to read it in one of your books."

"Ah, and what a book it might be! Only you would understand, knowing me so well. For the first time in my life I am in love. Every part of me is alive. Every part of me screams out for release from any containment. These past three days make up for a lifetime of deprivation."

"Does he feel the same way?"

"He says so. I won't believe otherwise."

"So, now what?"

"He will call me tomorrow night when he is back at the University. That conversation might seal my fate."

"I wish I could be a mouse on the wall so I could hear it all for myself."

"You know I will give you every detail. Sharing with you makes the special moments even more momentous."

"Make sure you use me as a character reference."

"You know me as a character better than anyone."

"My dear, dear friend, needless for me to say my only wish is for your happiness."

"My long time reserve wants me to hold back."

"Let yourself go."

"I will, dear heart. I do not want to jeopardize this chance."

They hugged again, and Cee left with Sherlock to head home. A long sigh followed as she closed the door behind her. "Bailey, you can't be involved in everything. Some books are for living."

Connor's mind raced in many directions during the drive back. He was totally enchanted by Celia. The author-laden ideas accompanied by a sharp wit and animated diagnosis of life and people, kept him spellbound. Combine this with a gentle and warm affectionate mannerism prompted by her natural outlook, and it was readily understandable that he was so charmed by her. If he had to put it into words, she had a childlike innocence and flare with a mature mind. Little wonder he was completely captivated.

A note from Kelly had been slipped under the door.

> *Welcome back, author man. I have finished reading*
> *your books while you were away. They are wonderful.*
> *I am fully qualified to be President of your fan club.*
> *Give me a call. I baked some blueberry muffins for*
> *you and will bring them over. Cheerio til then. K*

"This might be a problem," Connor thought to himself. It was important to call Celia first.

She answered after the first ring. "This better be who I hope it is."

"Guilty as charged."

"Normally, I am a patient person. It has been difficult waiting for something I was looking forward to so much."

"I do not disappoint those who depend on me."

"Sounds like a propitious way to lengthen your life."

"I hope my happiness as well."

"I know I am happy you called, just as I was happy to be with you."

"The one thought that is paramount is that life is too short and too fragile not to grab hold of happiness whenever you can."

"That is why I grabbed hold of you. I do not intend to let you go."

"I am an easy catch."

She chuckled. "All the better."

"Some might say we have a whirlwind romance."

"I don't feel that way. Do you?"

"No, I don't. There are some people you can know well in a short time. There are others you can never get to know."

"Exactly. The same goes for knowing yourself. I know, and I am neither doubtful or hesitant in saying it, that I love you."

"And I, sorting out what has happened and feeling your absence painfully, do love you."

"So, what next McGee?"

"Well, the Thanksgiving break is some five weeks away. I will be going down to have the Thanksgiving meal with my folks at the home. After that, I'll come your way for a few days."

"Not good enough to quench my thirst for your love. I can't wait that long to see you. I don't want to interfere with your teaching responsibilities, but maybe I can come up for a weekend before that. It's a two-day drive, but I have only my writing, Bailey, Becca, and Sherlock to hold me back. They will let me go, I am sure."

"That would be terrific, although I hate to see you do all of that driving."

"It is only the drive back that will be lonely."

They spent an extended time talking about a variety of subjects, each contributing a mixture of knowledge, experience, and candid opinion. Open discussions between people emotionally connected are facile and interesting.

After they hung up, Connor called Kelly. She hurried over with the muffins, accepting his excuse for not inviting her in that he was tired from the trip. She was perceptive to note that there were some subtle icicles around the edges, but she did not want to believe there could be any infringement on the budding relationship. She would await the report on the succulent treat, a foregone positive conclusion.

[T]he novelist now has to confront the larger problem of what the novel is even for – assuming it's not just another cultural widget.

Garth Risk Hallberg

A moment's insight is sometimes worth a life's experience.

Oliver Wendell Holmes

***

FOURTEEN

Since Connor had given the freshmen class a surprise test on the outside readings, presentation of the stories advising a younger sibling to avoid emotional hurt for others was postponed to this day. "Here are the tests back, and it is obvious many of you are not current in the readings. I will not count this test if you failed it, but there will be no second chances. If you passed, there will be extra credit."

There was an eager array of volunteers to read their stories. It was encouraging to see all of the raised hands. At least the art form was prompting some enthusiasm. He was careful to select a student who had not read aloud before.

Phyllis Ballenger, a frail looking woman with short brown hair, was recognized to read. Her voice belied the physical appearance, as it was cultured and resonant. Connor guessed there was some theatrical training and experience in her background.

TOUGH CHOICES

Having a younger sister is a mixed blessing.
She ranges from being a pest to the best.
Never asking me for advice, I was a bit
taken aback when she asked me whether
she should tell one of her friends that she
was adopted. She was sure she did not
know that, and it was only because of
helping out in the principal's office that
she happened to see the friend's file.

My reaction was swift. "There are times
when the doing of good is not doing anything
at all. It sounds inconsistent with friendship
to keep silent about something. It is not
your place to make that kind of disclosure.
Only her parents can and should do that.
After all, you do not know all of the facts
and circumstances, and it might be hurtful
all around to make known something that

may well be better off not known."

My sister hugged me, a hug that conveyed
an apparent understanding and agreement
of what I had said. Even after thinking about
it for awhile, my initial reaction was the best
one. It brought enforced learning to the
lesson that often the best decision is the
right one.

Connor nodded in approval. "Good Job, Phyllis. There can be and has been many a philosophical discussion concerning what is right as not always being best, but you complied with the assignment and it held my interest."

Another student who had not made a presentation before was recognized. Herschel Klein had thick black hair and riveting black eyes behind thick black-rimmed glasses. Black pants and a black shirt reminded Connor of the dark knight, or was it the dark night? His voice was raspy.

BULLYING EVIL

What is a bully?", my ten-year-old brother
asked before he entered my room. I
swiveled around in my desk chair and
noticed the serious look on his face. The
subject was more sensitive than he knew.
All I had to do was look into the past to
relive some harrowing moments. "A bully
is a lowly human being who preys on the
weaknesses of others, often hurting them
in many ways. It is really the bully who is
weak and insecure, as he belittles or harms
others to mask his own ineptness. Laws and
policy are getting stronger, but it probably
will never stop. The one who is bullied
usually is intimidated into a painful silence.
Is someone bullying you?"
"No," he answered tentatively. "I see it
going on all of the time."

"It would be a noble thing to do to report
it when you see it."
"They'll know."
"It is not easy. Yet, it won't end at all if
people stand by and do nothing."
"How can it be sure to end?"
"The last thing a bully wants is attention
from the authorities. His behavior is fueled
by the expectation that no one will do anything
about it. That's no bull!"

The class applauded, Connor joining in. "Nice job, Herschel. Bullying is a hot topic and one that can be complicated and controversial. Maybe, at some point, you can do a longer piece and cover it in the greater kind of detail that it deserves. Some subjects can stand extensive coverage even if duplicative."

Abigail Torrance was once again fidgeting in her chair, anxious to speak. Connor almost hoped her story would portray a lesson depicting that one cannot be first all of the time. She came up front as soon as he acknowledged her turn. She stood next to him peering into the student mass before her.

A MOMENT OF NEED

A moment of need creates an additional
dilemma. Who can I ask to help me? I
am not even sure of the nature and full
extent of the problem. Maybe it isn't even
a problem but just what I perceive as a
problem. Would that make a difference?
If it just involved me I could coast along
until things became clear, but there are
others affected. I thought my older sister
might help. She was the level-headed one
in the family.

I can still hear her words as if it were
yesterday, even though more than ten years
have passed. "Problems come in all shapes
and sizes as well as in varying degrees. If

your action or reaction involves others it
becomes even more complex. It is not fair
to make your problem theirs too. Think
things through, explore possible solutions,
and then proceed in stages so you can change
strategy along the way. A moment of need can
become a moment of deed."

Connor waited until the polite applause subsided. "Besides wandering away from the assignment, I think it would have been more interesting if the problem was defined rather than just taking a philosophical approach. You do want to make readers think. Yet, you do not want to confuse them or lead them too far away from what you are trying to portray. It might even be better to lay out the problem or gist of the content and let their imagination fill in the blanks. Hemingway said that his best short story had just six words: For sale: baby shoes, never worn. As haunting as the images may arise, the craft of the writer has amply been displayed. You write well, Abigail. The secret is to keep the reader's attention and interest in mind."

Next up was Ronnie DeWitt, and Connor was prepared for the young man's splurge at humor.

WHY ME?

The last thing I want or need is for someone
to ask me for advice. Especially my eleven-
year old brother asking me about girls. After
all, I need advice in that department myself.
There was no escaping when he cornered me,
looked at me sheepishly, and blurted out, "Can
an eleven-year old girl become pregnant?"
"I don't think you want to find that out?"
"Why not?"
"There is one thing worse than an eleven-
year old mother, and that is an eleven-year
old father. I don't want to be a nineteen
year-old uncle either."
"She asked me for sex."
"It is against the law. Besides, do you even
know about sex?"

"I thought I'd learn by trying it."
"It's not like riding a bike. There is much more
than just the physical part. There are mental
and emotional aspects. I dare say she does not
know about it either."
"Can't we learn together?"
"I know this is tough to grasp, but it would not
be fair to her or to you."
"How so?"
"The consequences, little brother, can be
long-lasting. Those consequences can only be
faced when there is maturity and financial stability,
not to mention that it can eliminate most other
life choices. Tell her it will be much better when
you are both older."
His glance went down to the floor. "It is too late."

"I expected something humorous," Connor spoke slowly. "This was serious."

"I figured that being serious once and awhile makes my funny efforts more hilarious."

"We'll find that out soon enough."

When a book elevates your mind, and
inspires you with noble thoughts, you
require nothing else to judge it; it is
a good and masterly work.

Jean de la Bruyere
Characters (1688)

Living the past is a dull and lonely
business; looking back strains the
neck muscles, causing you to bump
into people not going your way.

Edna Ferber

***

FIFTEEN

On his way to the workshop, Connor recalled the previous evening when he had asked Kelly to go for a walk. Before telling her about Celia, he raved about the blueberry muffins, as they were truly delicious. The unsettling image of the hurt look on her faced stayed with him.

Valiantly, Kelly had joked about the muffins, declaring they were a means to bring them closer together and not prompt him to seek a different baker. She was disappointed, but she would not give up on him or the potential of the kind of relationship she wanted. She would just linger in the wings and hope that Connor would eventually see that true romance and lasting involvement was with her. She knew she had as much to offer him as any other woman might. If she had known that Celia was not attractive and older than Connor, her resolve would have been further fortified.

Ken Trollop was the first to read the story he wrote over the two weeks the workshop had to prepare a short, short story without any subject limitations. Ken had a full beard, unusual for his young years, although he might not be as young as Connor thought. It was no easy task to tell a person's age with so many factors involved. Some people age long before they need to while others are treated kindly by the advancing years. His voice was deep and rich.

THE SURPRISE

Why do people choose to surprise someone who does not like surprises? One theory, perhaps, is that really everyone likes a surprise and the disdain is feigned as a disguise to enhance the surprise effect. Not Elroy Perchant. He only desired an orderly life, and that meant everything should be organized and predictable. Even as a youngster, he did not enjoy unanticipated gifts or other attempts at surprise to alter his world.

Of course, his boss at work did not know of this peculiarity. So, he planned a surprise office party to announce Elroy's promotion and special cash bonus. When the event unfurled, Elroy was stuck

in what appeared to be a tortuous dilemma. Would
he graciously fall into the festivity knowing that he
had worked so hard for the advancement? Or,
would he be true to himself and denounce the manner
in which his boss unwittingly chose to hold an office
celebration? If you were Elroy, what would you do?

The class applause was enthusiastic before Connor offered his comments. "Ken, that sure was interesting. Most readers, however, would probably prefer that Elroy's decision be laid out rather than having to do that on their own, although they would either champion or reject such an outcome. Basically, that means what they would do if they were in his shoes but without the strain of being left dangling. An author wants the reader to closely identify with the character and agonize over any decision the character makes. It is a fine line though to put them on the spot to make it completely their decision."

Gloria Feld was the next to read her story, Connor guessing it would be romantic in nature and that her mother was sent a copy.

A KISS GOOD-BYE

Her body trembled. It was hard to tell if it was
from excitement or dread. Why is it that a
moment you look forward to suddenly takes on
ominous features? It seems the longer you have
to wait for something the more your imagination
opens doors better left closed.

Fred Ellis lived down the street from her all of
of their lives. They had gone to the same schools
and being the same age they were in the same
grade. She had worshipped him since she was
nine. He had always been friendly but there had
never been any romantic feelings or overtures
on his part. He was not handsome although he
was a really nice guy. He treated everyone with
respect. Bridgett liked that.

Tonight was a going-away party for him. He had

joined the marines upon their graduation from
high school. Since her parents were friends with
his parents, she was also invited to the party. He
would undoubtedly kiss all of the females a fond
farewell. All of these years she dreamed of him
kissing her, and it would now finally happen. But,
what kind of kiss would it be? Would everyone
be watching? Would he guide her to some secluded
spot and declare a newly discovered love for her?
Would it be a peck on the cheek or a full kiss on
the lips? What would she do? What could she say?

For all of the questions, the most important one arose
later. Why do the things you anticipate as being so
wonderful often turn out to be disappointing?

Yes, Fred kissed her. It was on the lips and held for
several seconds. It mattered not that all in attendance
observed it. It was a nothing. Mushy would be an
apt description. It left her speechless, not from its
hoped for desirable results but because it was totally
blah. There might have been a greater impact if she
had kissed a wet towel She had never heard of a
person drowning when a dream bubble bursts, but
she now had no doubt that it was possible. A moment
of reality can destroy years of dreams. Good-bye to
a kiss good-bye.

Connor joined in the applause. "Your mother certainly has competition. It is rewarding for the reader as well when an author conveys ordinary human thoughts and feelings. When writing and reading join forces, it is a satisfying shared experience. Nice job, Gloria."

Gordon Anterwick stood when he was recognized, eagerly ready to read his story. Connor had not noticed before that the young man had a tattoo on the side of his neck. Partially covered by his shirt, it was not completely visible although it appeared to be an animal. He could never understand why people chose to be tattooed, especially young people. Perhaps, he was just too much of a prude, but it just seemed to be an ugly tainting of the skin and there would be a better choice to show individual expression.

THE VISION

He saw it only for a fleeting second, too brief to make out what it was. Yet, it was mesmerizing. What did it mean? He had never had a vision before, and until now he believed such was not possible. A few days later he saw it again. This time it was longer and clearer. It was a human form, a woman in a flowing white gown. He could not make out the features of the face. It was several weeks before he saw it again. It held longer and was sharp enough for him to see that it was his mother She had died eight years earlier. What was he to make of it?

Two days passed and he saw it once again, longer and brighter than before. In her hand was a knife with blood dripping from it. Was it a warning for his own death by violent means? As far as he knew, he had no enemies. Would it then be by a random act? He refused to live in fear, but he would be vigilant about all he did and wherever he would go.

Months passed and there were no further visions. After a year he had just about written it off as an offshoot of his overactive imagination when as he was returning to his apartment he saw a blood-stained knife on the sidewalk. No one else was around. He looked up the alley and saw a woman slumped over on the ground next to a dumpster. Her white dress was soaked in blood. He pulled out his cell phone and punched in 911. Within minutes the ambulance and police arrived. The woman was taken to the hospital and it turned out that even another five minute delay and it would have been too late to save her. She survived.

The young woman was the cashier at the local movie theater. A thief thought she had the night's receipts with her as she headed home. Finding

*her without money, in frustration the thief stabbed
her and dragged her into the alley.*

*He visited her at the hospital often during her
recovery. Then they dated. The greatest impact
for him was that her name was Irene, his mother's
name. He had no more visions. Had he seen his
mother, the white gown, and the knife so that he
might save Irene? Or, was it all just an uncanny
coincidence?*

"Talk about an over-active imagination," Connor offered as the applause subsided. "Where do you get your ideas?"

Gordon gave a broad smile. "I just pretend I am watching a movie. The action comes on its own."

"Did you see many movies as a youngster?"

"Every chance I could get."

"And, I bet, you want to work in the movie industry some day?"

"Exactly."

"Figures."

Gwen Jenner was next, and she did not begin until she was sure she had everyone's full attention. Connor was again amazed at her booming voice belying her frail physical appearance.

A BRIDGE OF REGRETS

*Forget a regret! Good advice because a regret can
eat away at you and cause unnecessary anguish. What
happened cannot be changed. If you have a series of
regrets, each will intrude on the other and the only
thing you can do is build a bridge with them, a shaky
one at best. I speak from experience. I have second-
guessed many of the actions I took in my life, compelling
me to regret what I did do or did not do. For example,
my older sister wrote beautiful poetry. I stole one of them
and pretended to others that I created it. Not only do I
believe now that others knew such was well beyond my
ability, after the initial charade there was no sense of*

accomplishment or satisfaction. To this day, I am not
sure if my sister ever knew of my dastardly deed. She
never said anything, and maybe she felt sorry for me.
For what was a small victory of sorts, a huge regret
has loomed ever since.

In high school, my best friend and I had a crush on the
same boy. He was a bit shy and he confided in me that
he liked my friend and wanted me to tell her that. I never
did hoping that if he got no response from her he would
then turn his attention to me. It did not work out that way.
I betrayed a friendship, a valuable relationship, for a
selfish whim. I have deeply regretted that since then.

There have been cowardly and dishonorable deeds,
none of which I am proud of. The really sad part is that
I am not sure I have learned a lesson or that if the
opportunity arose I would not choose a path based
solely on self-need and satisfaction. And, I would
probably regret such long thereafter. A bridge of
regrets is an architectural anomaly. It starts from
nowhere and goes nowhere.

The class applause indicated approval. Connor offered that a story can convey a strong moral lesson. "If that was a true story, I hope you do not regret revealing it. Confession is good for the soul." He had a feeling that Gwen was baring some truths, at least her perception of them. "Most people think of writing in terms of spelling and grammar. Actually, as is so evident by the writings we do and hear, writing is a cross-section of all subjects. I dare say the entire college curriculum enters into the text and ideas conveyed."

There was time for one more story to be read. Connor called on Bernadette La Rouche. Her French accent gave added emphasis to her story. She came to the front of the class and read from the gold-colored sheets of paper she held.

THE CHAMBERMAID'S DAUGHTER

One need not travel to a foreign country to experience
a clash of cultures, a culture shock. There is enough

*diversity in this nation to be exposed to such a
phenomenon here. One such a happening was
brought home to Rodney Carter when as a big city
boy he took a summer job as a waiter at a country
inn. The housekeeping employees were recruited
from the small town nearby.*

*One day, Rodney was asked by the owner to go to
one of the rooms to help move a dresser. The most
beautiful girl he had ever seen was there making up
the bed. Her name was Gretchen and she was
helping her mother with the rooms on that floor.
They talked for awhile, and he asked her out on
a date.*

*They dated for several weeks but grew uncomfortable
with one another. She, as a small town girl, was wary
of the reputation of big city boys, and was timid about
the display of too much affection. He grew tired of
her stiffness and reserve. She would not relax and just
be herself. The allure of beauty tarnished with a
distance that could not be breached. He had the sense
that he was a form of trophy that she just wanted to
brag to her friends about. Her aloofness became
boring. A relationship cannot have a future when
its present is restrained and undefined. The setting
and experience of the participants were too far
apart. Never the twain shall meet. The chambermaid's
daughter was just a fading memory.*

Connor nodded as the applause ceased. "Good story, Bernadette. It would certainly make an intriguing book as there is room, excuse the pun, for an extended analysis of the characters and their environment. I can tell you all enjoyed this unbridled opportunity to express yourselves. Keep in mind that most assignments will be your choice, so keep a notebook handy to jot down ideas that often come at strange and unexpected moments. It has been told that many authors keep pads by their beds to write down dreams which may evaporate in the light of day. The mind has no boundary except the one we purposely impose on it. Let your spirit loose, and as you revisit what you may think about and write about even a change can also be unrestricted. There might be so many drafts of a story that the initial one may no longer be recognizable. As a variation, for the next assignment write a story using the following last sentence: The past is no prediction of the future.

The pen is the tongue of the mind.

Cervantes

The ink of the scholar is more sacred than the blood of the martyr.

Mohammed

There is no distance on this earth as far away as yesterday.

Robert Nathan

SIXTEEN

Cee left Sherlock with Bee at the studio. They hugged warmly. So much can be conveyed by a hug.

"I am just an artist and often at a loss for words," Bee pronounced softly after the embrace. "My heart goes with you wherever you go and whatever you do. Opportunities for happiness are for those who take advantage of them. You leave here with love, and may you find what you so richly deserve. No matter what happens, there is a refuge here. Come back with or without him."

Cee clasped Bee's hand. "Those are beautiful words and precious thoughts, my true and loyal friend. I am optimistic about this visit. Connor is encouraging and he will not let me down. I feel that in my heart just as I feel and know the love in my heart for you. I will not jeopardize this chance. I know I do not go alone. Everything you have done and do for me is greatly appreciated, and I know I have your full love and support."

"I've done what I can and am ready for this Connor fella to take over. But, not completely." Her chuckle was genuine.

"Sounds like it would work for me."

Cee stopped at a motel a little more than halfway through the trip. She was calmer than she thought she would be. She looked at it as if she was writing a book. Bailey, the sophisticated woman was always in control, even in situations where so much rested on the outcome. As much as she desired an advantageous result, the situation would usually be manipulated to favor her position. A restless night belied much of the self-confidence. Could she believe in Connor as much as she believed in herself?

Knocking on his door, her heart raced ahead as a result of the built-up anticipation she had kept in check. Seeing his warm smile and feeling the firm embrace, her world was just in the place she wanted it to be. Even Bailey would have been satisfied.

Holding her, Connor realized he had missed her even more than he thought. The physical and emotional fit was magical. They kissed and the salt from her tears touched his lips. As authors, it was apparent a new and important chapter had begun. As the main characters in the epoch, they wanted to savor one page at a time. The passage needs to experience the systematic glide through each and every sentence, stopping to fully partake of the special meaningful thoughts and expressions.

Except for a few walks shortened by a continuous cold rain, they stayed in spending the time as an offshoot of the shared love. Cooking together was particularly enjoyable, symbolizing closeness in the ordinary actions of life. They exchanged gifts of their books, prompting numerous discussions on many facets of writing. A nexus exists between writers even if the creative efforts produce different products.

"I wish I could stay here with you," Celia murmured one evening as they shared a succulent dinner. "Better yet, I wish you could be with me in Plainview. It is peaceful there, almost as if the troubling world cannot touch it. The people are friendly, kind, and considerate. You would love Becca and her family. I just know they would love you. My home is set up for endless writing."

"Food for thought, for sure. I'll get a taste of it at Thanksgiving after I visit my parents. I have this commitment here until June and it is time well spent. I wish you could sit in on my classes. Talent and growing absorption in writing are evident. As much as I love writing, it is uplifting to inspire others to write."

"Yet, you do not want to neglect your own writing. My home, as small as it is, would be conducive to your writing. During the quiet and any difficult times, I would love you fiercely. It would be a loving transition to our home."

"That might prompt me to be in a funk perpetually."

"It will also catapult you to new and greater heights. I know it will be that way for me with you at my side."

"I certainly might tire of the teaching role by the end of the year, but right now it is quite engrossing. I have been invited to some book conferences too, and there is one between Thanksgiving and Christmas in New York City."

"There is room for it all, my sweets. You know I am not talking about tomorrow, although such is an appealing idea. When the time is ripe, it will be there for us to grab hold of."

"I can't understand how such a sensible and entreating woman never married."

"And I can't understand how a bevy of women let you out of their clutches."

He grinned broadly. "I suppose they did not want to cross paths with you and Bailey and risk a severe brow beating."

"Darling man, my intellect is my most powerful weapon."

"Dearest woman, intellect is just one of your many weapons in a complete arsenal."

"After you read my books, you'll have to choose between me and Bailey."

"I can't have you both?"

"And be constantly outnumbered?"

"Good point." He reached for her hand and gave it a gentle squeeze. "I settle for you."

"Don't rush to judgment. Bailey is alluring and powerful."

"Pales in the light of your attributes."

"Do you feel close to any of your characters?"

"There are different individuals in each book. Yet, as only another author knows, there is in each of them a little bit of the actual, the desired, and the imagined me. Roll them all together and it is the past, present, and future Connor at your service."

She squeezed his hand, the happiness overflowing in her mind and spirit. "Most of the me I wanted to be is Bailey. Now, I realize the me that I am is the better person because she could only pretend to have you."

"Yes, but having a character like Bailey affords the luxury of seeing and knowing yourself as well as affirming that your own hopes and dreams are possible."

"A short while ago I may have disputed that. Now, I agree."

A gentle caress on his arm completed, he continued speaking in a low tone. "I could never have had this kind of conversation with that bevy of women. You are easy to talk with as to be with. A treasure you are I am quick to add."

"You sure are a flatterer."

"At a book fair about a year ago, I was on a panel with a book reviewer. He made the statement that really set me off. He said that a good writer doesn't give answers. I argued that good writers should give answers appropriate for the characters and allude to the possibility of other answers if such is the case. That way all kinds of readers can be satisfied. Some readers need it all laid out for them; others need clues to grasp. Good writers come in all disguises just as good readers come in assorted combinations. I surmised that he thought if you give an answer you are insulting the intelligence of the reader. The challenge is to make the reader reach beyond the answer."

"I buy all of that, sterling professor. In my mysteries I try to meld the obvious with the not-so-apparent conclusions. The last thing I want is for someone to drop my book because it is hard to understand what is happening or why."

"There is a whole cross-section of readers of a book while there is only the one author. A battle of nerves and wits."

"For sure, as we can attest to, writers are a breed unto themselves."

"I like to think all creative people are bound by a Gordian knot."

"As I am to you."

"And I to you."

By the time Celia left, there was additional comfort in knowing that any uncertainties had dissipated. In their place was the even and calm flow of tested feelings.

The trip back was easy enough, and Cee was bursting to tell Bee all of the events. Happiness is grand in itself and yet when it is shared with those we love it is a further abundant joy. Becca was entranced by the description of all the happenings and feelings, and when she hugged Cee anew that conveyed the euphoria. She certainly trusted Cee's interpretation and judgment. But there was still the nagging trouble spot that a long-term dear friend is cautious about. The thought formed in her mind, If this Connor fellow disappoints and hurts her, I'll have to kill him.

*Every author in some degree portrays
himself in his works, even if it is
against his will.*

Johan Wolfgang Von Goethe

*And choose an author as you choose
a friend.*

Wentworth Dillon

*The book is a living voice. It is an
intellect to which one still listens.*

Samuel Smiles

SEVENTEEN

The freshman class was to prepare a paragraph ending with the sentence: The past is no prediction of the future. Connor was anxious to see how they handled it. This was a variation of the old party game where the punch line of a joke is given and people have to make up the joke itself.

Herschel Klein, in his usual all black attire was the first to be recognized for participation. He paused for an instant before speaking.

> *He identified closely with the night. That is why he chose to dress in black. His deepest thoughts were dark. Life had been unkind to him and he was going to display his suffering to the world. There was no reason to step out of the darkness. The light behind the bolted door was for others, not for him. To smile was to show weakness. To have hope or faith was to deny reality. To listen to his professor's hollow pronouncement was to discard the lesson so brutally learned. "The past is no prediction of the future."*

"Wow!" Connor was genuinely surprised. After the applause subsided, he offered his reaction. "I was upbeat when I came in today. Now, I am dejected. I do hope this was pure fiction. Life is far too short to succumb to a bad experience or to cast a pale over each day."

Herschel knew it was pure fiction and that he only dressed in black because it kept people guessing. He was not going to open any window to his soul. "I give people what I think they want. It is easier to explain my affinity to black by offering them what they think they know."

"Far be it for me to stir the waters, but perhaps you do not give people enough credit. It was a powerful paragraph even though it was depressing."

Abigail Torrence was next although she had wanted to be first. Connor noted a mischievous twinkle in her eye.

I liked what I heard from the author as she
described the book she had written. As
soon as I could I bought it. I figured I
would enjoy it, and I did. I couldn't wait
until her next book was released. The
expectancy just kept growing over the
two years that followed. The new book
was totally disappointing, and I discarded
it after reading only a few chapters. The
past is no prediction of the future.

The usual applause followed. Connor was quick to remark. "That was good Abagail, and I especially liked that the subject pertained to writing. An author who has written a well-liked book is under great pressure to match or exceed that accomplishment. Some truly have only one book in them and all of their talent and imagination is spent in that opus. A publisher needs to accept the responsibility that a second or later work should stand on its own and not be greedy that a past success will lead to strong initial sales. It is self-defeating in the end. It can be quite devastating to an author."

Dylan Forrester was a new volunteer and Connor was quick to recognize her. The young woman had short red hair with bangs down to her blue eyes. A white bulky sweater came down long over faded blue jeans. Her voice was full and melodic.

There is much in this world to be upset by
and concerned about. The more she read
of the good old days, the more she wished
she had been part of that tranquil and slow
paced time rather than caught in the
instant rewards mentality of the current
generation. Those days, unfortunately,
are gone forever. The current upheavals
and catastrophic challenges might even
be totally different in the world of tomorrow.
The past is no prediction of the future.

"A good and concise paragraph, Dylan," Connor pronounced as the applause quieted. "It can be a battle to convey an idea wrapped up in a single paragraph."

Another new reader was next. Marsha Henson was a rather tall young woman with straight auburn hair and piercing brown eyes. A white satin blouse was tucked into a plaid skirt with high white knee socks.

> *"Follow your dreams," my father said to me*
> *just before he died. There was no time for a*
> *discussion of the problems inherent in*
> *dreaming. A dream is free; reality quite*
> *costly. Then, there is the daunting problem*
> *of interpreting a dream. I know he meant*
> *that I should not unduly restrain myself.*
> *There are enough conditions imposed by*
> *society that amount to barriers. There are*
> *also all of the uncertainties found in human*
> *frailty. On top of all of that there is the truism*
> *that the past is no prediction of the future.*

Connor waited for the applause to end. "It is sound advice to follow your dreams. Dreams have no boundaries, and dreams lead us to paths that might not be traveled otherwise. They are a prime ingredient for writing. Dreaming sets the spirit free and produces a flying pen."

Ed Shatlee was the last to read on that day. Ed was a short and stocky man, and the blue shirt clashed with his brown pants. Connor had the idea that the young man did not care how he looked.

> *Like the discovery of a new flavor of ice*
> *cream, he could not get enough of her.*
> *Once he noticed her, his eyes were riveted*
> *to her every movement. What was the*
> *allure? She was not especially attractive*
> *and her clothing was not appealing. It was*
> *her bearing, the way she carried herself.*
> *It was just like his Aunt Jennie who had*
> *always presented an imposing figure of*
> *purpose and confidence. Aunt Jennie*
> *had been his most favorite person in the*
> *world. She had died before she reached*
> *fifty and he had missed her terribly. Now,*
> *this single ordinary observation had opened*
> *the floodgates of melancholy. Is there a*

secret connection between people of
different generations? Are there characteristics
and involvements that emerge anew in people?
Is it a fallacy to state that the past is no
prediction of the future?

Connor nodded his approval throughout the applause. "Ed, that was a meaningful paragraph. It held my attention and was thought-provoking. I liked that you varied the last sentence by turning it into a question. Well, folks, you are from what I can tell on your way to making your own personal inroad into the world of literature, even if it is only for your own enjoyment and satisfaction. More power to you all!"

No tears in the writer, no tears in the reader.

George Moore

A word is dead
When it is said,
Some say.
I say it just begins
To live that day.

Emily Dickinson

Tis' better to live your life
imperfectly than to imitate
someone else's perfectly.

Elizabeth Gilbert

EIGHTEEN

These were dismal days for Kelly. She could not get Connor out of her amorous thoughts. It did not help that she embellished her feelings in the daily telephone talks with her family, and she even made up stories to bolster her imaginary flowing romantic involvement. She was torn between doing nothing and making some overtures to entice a relationship. She did not want him to forget her.

Events dictated her behavior. She was walking Gildersleeve just as Connor was hiking up from the campus. As he approached, her agile mind concocted a greeting. "I thought you had moved out or are avoiding me because you did not like my baking."

"How are you, Kelly. As is obvious, I have not moved and your baking talent is etched in gold." She sure was an attractive woman, and Connor quickly dismissed any notion to compare her to Celia. Yet, within that dismissal the germ of a comparison flickered.

Kelly pressed on. "I have more than half an apple pie left. McIntosh apples are plentiful now and I use them in pies and for making applesauce. Why don't you come over later for dessert and I'll make sure your body and mind are nourished."

Connor 's inclination was to refuse the invitation. Yet, a warm memory seeped into his mind of the evenings that he and Dorie would stop at the Hospitality House after seeing an old movie at the theater. It was a favorite restaurant of theirs on the avenue and if they had any extra money they would have their legendary apple pie with ice cream on it. That was considered an ultimate treat and they savored every morsel. "That sure is kind of you, but I won't be able to stay long. I have a ton of work crushing down on me."

Kelly smiled, pulling her shoulders back so that her ample breasts were more pronounced through the sweatshirt. "That is fine. I have a stack of papers to grade."

The gesture was not lost on Connor. Again, perhaps because of the inherent weakness in his private character, he could not help to compare her attributes with Celia's small chest and poor posture.

After making and digesting scrambled eggs, he went over to Kelly's place. He would telephone Celia when he returned.

Kelly had on one of her favorite outfits, sure that it would be to her advantage. She set the table in the dining room with autumn symbols and figurines. Around each plate upon which she would serve the pie there were colorful leaves and miniature pumpkins. When she opened the door, she hugged him firmly and holding it at length. "I am so glad you could make it over. I am warming the pie up. I am serving it with pumpkin ice cream.'

He had to admit that he enjoyed such a hug. "Sounds great." He glanced at the decorated table. "You sure do have a creative design touch. I get so involved with the world of writing that I tend to overlook that a special flare can exist in so many other activities."

She stood as close to him as she could intoxicated by his presence. "Another aspect of coming from a large family. We not only marked each holiday in traditional fashion, the seasons brought changes in how the house was decorated. My mother would go overboard in the kitchen."

Conversation flowed as they ate. Connor had to admit the pie was the best he ever had. It was easy to be with Kelly, not in a romantic way but as if she was an old friend. For Kelly, it was the projection of a love interest with family potential which generated the laughter and conversation.

As he was leaving, he bent forward to kiss her on the cheek. She craftily moved her head so that the kiss was on her lips. It lingered there to her delight and to his amazement.

Talking to the family later that evening, she did not have to make up any stories. The rising hope in her heart broadcasted her glowing report.

An apple pie intoxication was the way he figured it. There was really little danger that it would get out-of-hand. When he telephoned Celia and their conversation drifted to the intellectual and emotional arenas they frequented, the taste of apple pie was substituted by the liquor of love.

I have been successful probably because
I have always realized that I know nothing
about writing and have merely tried to
tell an interesting story entertainingly.

Edgar Rice Burroughs

A writer never has a vacation. For a
writer life consists of either writing or
thinking about writing.

Eugene Jonesco

Daniel Hill Zafren

*When you are born you were crying and
everyone else was smiling. Live your life
so at the end, you're the one who is
smiling and everyone else is crying.*

Ralph Waldo Emerson

***

NINETEEN

The Thanksgiving holiday break arrived, too quickly for some and not fast enough for others. Blantyre University was converted into a ghost town. For an outside observer it would be an eerie sight and sensation, repeated countless number of times across the nation.

Connor spent two days with his parents and was their guest at the Thanksgiving dinner at the home. It was a most pleasant visit. The weather was warm enough for several strolls around the grounds. Connor told them at length about his students and the budding romantic involvement with Celia. They knew when he was ready he would bring her around to meet them. The only girl he had ever brought home was Dorie, and they well knew the passion that relationship had engendered.

The parents were doing well. They looked and acted contented with life's autumnal respite. His mother had even organized a musical presentation that was enjoyed by all. There was a piano in the great room, the gathering place for the home's special events. She was in her element. He left them with a full heart to spend several days with Celia. The heart would need to expand even further.

Cee spent Thanksgiving day with Bee and the family as she always had. She brought her traditional green bean casserole and rolls that she had to go over to Beaverton, the nearest town with a bakery.

Celia had given detailed directions to the house. She was fidgety awaiting his arrival. A mystery of love is that it can either engender great patience or impatience. It was Sherlock's bark announcing someone approaching the house that sent her flying through the front door and into his arms. Her tight embrace nearly crushed the bouquet of flowers he was carrying.

She held on to him as she showed him the house. Celia had enhanced the charm of an older home with family heirlooms and a writer's design for inspiration and production. Connor detected her inimitable touch throughout, and he was especially entranced by Becca's paintings, particularly since he had already seen them on the covers of Celia's books. The glow of pride and excitement showed on her face. He could easily see living in this house, although he could probably live anywhere with her.

After spending some quiet private time, they went to Bee's house for dinner. As Cee had surmised, Connor was charmed by Bee and the family, and they all readily accepted him. Bee noted all of the special attention Connor paid to her friend and it was difficult to restrain tears coming to her eyes. When an elusive moment becomes real it can be overwhelming.

Later that night as they lay in each other's arms, Celia stroked his cheek. "My sweet man, I have read all of your books. Let me rephrase that. I have devoured your books. You write beautifully. I wish I had a smidgeon of your talent. In comparison, my books are just fluff."

"I have not gotten to read them yet, but they are in the priority pile on my desk. I am sure you do not give yourself enough credit. Your books are wildly popular. Witness the reaction from the audience at the panel we were on."

"My favorite book is An Illusive Intrusion. And, my favorite part which I have read so many times I have committed it to memory. Maturity, in the sense of realizing what is truly important in your life to make you happy, came late for him. It was not that he squandered his youth. It was just that the beliefs and people that he wanted included in his makeup were gone before he knew it and much too late for him to recapture. Is it your own life you were describing?"

His fingers clutched at her hand. "As I tell my students, probably all writing has roots in some form of reality, or at least in a personal interpretation of that reality tinged with imagination, expectations, and hallucinations."

She chuckled covering his hand with her own. "That did not answer the question, but I liked it anyway."

"Would you like this answer any better? It is me and not me."

"Then who are you?"

"I am who I am."

"Am you in love with me?"

"That is now a major part of who I am."

"Whoever you are, you are for me."

"Sold."

"And delivered?"

"Special delivery."

The next day, they walked to Bee's studio. Becca hugged Connor as earnestly as she did Cee. Captivated by the paintings, it was obvious to Connor that creativity can take many forms. A painting can be a story. The more he stared at the paintings he was entranced by the expert use of lines and colors. The longer he looked the more he saw. That same sort of magic can exist with books. Whenever he read a book for a second time, including his own, he got more out of it. There were finer points and ideas to dwell upon.

Days pass far too quickly when happy and meaningful times are shared. On the night before he was to leave, a soothing calm engulfed them delineating the contours of the relationship. It would be just a few weeks and he would return to this special closeness with her. He would also take her to meet his parents. The interval would be hectic with catching up on student progress, planning assignments for the Christmas holiday, and having to participate on the panel discussion at the literary conference in New York City.

As Celia watched his car pull away, the tears symbolized an eternal emotional mystery. A blend of happiness and the sense of separation, no matter how brief it might be, urged the tears to form. All of this was actually a new feeling and its impact was powerful. Even Bailey would have been touched.

After hugging, Bee could not restrain herself. "I have a title for a book you need to write.......Miss Wonderful Meets Mr. Right. I am so happy for you. Perfect people in a perfect match."

"I think this book will write itself. He is charmed by you, your paintings, and your family. That is very important to me. Equally important, I think he is alright with the idea of living here."

"Has he mentioned marriage?"

"Let's not push the formalities. He wants to finish his teaching responsibilities and that sure is a testament to his character."

"Again, I am just so happy for you. Your happiness is my happiness. I think I might burst."

"Please do not do that, I need you."

Celia closed her eyes. If this were just a dream she did not want to wake up. Yet, it was not a dream. It was the fulfillment of her being.....at long last!

Put down everything that comes into your
head and then you're a writer. But an author
is one who judges his own stuff's worth,
without pity, and destroys most of it.

Colette

Life is not measured by the number of breaths
you take, but by the moments that take your
breath away.

Maya Angelou

***

TWENTY

At the workshop, Bernadette La Rouche was the first to be called upon to read her creative effort, Connor having set no boundaries as to subject, length, or style. The French accent provided an additional emphasis to a voice best described as melodious

DREAMS OF DYING

*Nothing has been the same since I dreamt I
died. Perhaps, I am actually dead. I dreamt
I fell asleep at the wheel while driving one
night. I could sense the car veering off the road
but I was powerless to turn the steering wheel
to correct it. My eyes were stuck closed. It
was an awful sensation, and then I stopped
feeling anything. A snowy television-like screen
that had appeared before my eyes went blank*

*Eight days later I dreamt I had a heart attack.
There was a tightness in my chest, pain radiated
from my neck down my arms, and there was defined
tingling in my fingers. I felt my body stiffen and I
forced myself into a fetal position. Then there was
nothing except the sound of my breathing which was
very pronounced as if it were in an echo chamber.   It
became distant and slower and then ceased.*

*Since those dreams I have not been able to concentrate
on anything and my power of reasoning has abandoned
me. Things that I have valued seem worthless, and I
cannot enjoy what I used to relish. Even eating is a
purely mechanical function. There is no taste, and I
I cannot differentiate between hot and cold.*

*I did research and asked around about the meaning of
dreaming of dying. Of course, no one dares to*

pronounce that such is an actual prediction of death or other dire consequence. That might lead to a form of panic. Rather, the consensus of opinion is that such a dream indicates the person is under a great deal of stress. Hog wash I say to that! I am not under any stress. My theory is that certain events cannot be readily explained away and society under those conditions makes an effort to keep it all as benign as possible.

So, what am I to conclude? It has prompted an obsession about death causing a diminished form of living. The really important question is how long will this last? Is it merely an emotional earthquake to nudge me to change who I am and what I want? Is it a catharsis? Is it an acknowledgement of my inner self that I should start things anew? Or, is it simply trying to convey a basic lesson that I should not put myself at risk by driving when I am sleepy and making an effort to live a healthy lifestyle?

For certain, it has led me to question things about myself. That is a positive if it leads to a constructive end. What if it raises such doubts and fears that I conclude only death is an escape? That would bring me full circle. I am reluctant to close my eyes. If my own dying is a torment, what if I should dream a loved one dies? If my own dream has caused my death, might it cause the death of another?

Scary stuff seeps into my thoughts. Will that transfer to my dreams? I am afraid to dream. I might just as well be dead because this is no way to live.

There was no applause, as an eerie silence hung over the throng. Connor felt compelled to say something. "Young lady, that was a deep and somewhat troubling story. I do hope it was just a fictionalized flight of your imagination. The interpretation of dreams is complicated and controversial. One should not get carried away with it."

Bernadette flashed her brown eyes in his direction. "I actually had those dreams, but it has not had the profound effect on me as I described. It just opened a plethora of subjects to think about."

"Are you sure that is all it is? Your effort reveals a collage of feelings."

"Not to worry. The French are famous for exaggeration and embellishment." She was the only one who laughed at her attempt at humor.

Len wheeler spoke next. Despite his youthful face, Connor noted a certain sadness around the eyes. His voice was raspy.

FRIENDSHIP AS A NEGATIVE

We hear and read about friendship as being
wonderful. T'aint necessarily so!

When I was twelve, I had a best friend.
We did everything together. We swore
we would be friends forever and do whatever
the other might ask. Well, that was fine for
awhile. The dilemma arose the first time
it was put to the test.

We walked to and from school with two girls
our age who lived on the same street. My friend
confided in me he had a crush on one of the girls,
the prettier of the two. Secretly, I also liked her
a lot. Instead of being honest and forthright
about it all, I did what I believed the friendship
demanded. I stepped aside for him since he had
confided in me first. So, I announced I liked the
other girl. Being young and way too foolish, we
pressed the girls into revealing which of us they
liked best. They finally confessed they both liked
one of us, and that turned out to be me. When all
was said and done, the four of us were miserable
and I was sure I felt the worst. Small potatoes you
probably say to yourself. Nothing is small when
you live a lie.

And, it did not end there. Rather the rewards of

*closeness and concern, any friendship I tried to
encourage ended in betrayal, treachery, or greed.
Who needs a friend anyway? Each person is his
own best friend, and that is all there need be.*

Polite applause greeted the finish. Connor shook his head. "If I was in a good mood today, these two stories have taken care of that. Len, I hope this was pure fiction. I would hate to see anyone, especially a young person, write off one of life's most rewarding gifts. A friend is a special blessing, and when life becomes difficult it is usually a friend who can ease the way by sharing the burden and offering encouragement. It is a grand human achievement, and is akin to love. I feel for anyone who does not find love and friendship."

Len displayed a puzzled look. "It is just a story and not my philosophy. Although I must admit it takes great effort and a risky chance to place trust in others."

"Perhaps, but well worth it."

Gwen Jenner shuffled her papers and smoothed down her blonde hair before she began speaking. The theatrical training showed in her perfect diction and appropriate inflections in her voice.

THE HAPPY WANDERER

*Music serves many purposes and can represent
a life at peace or unrest. When I was twelve
my grandfather gave me a music box. It was
in the form of an old English cottage, and when
you lifted the thatched roof it played the tune
"The Happy Wanderer." It is one of my most
cherished possessions. I closely associate with
that tune.*

*I have had many experiences for one as young as
I am. Some might say I flit from one thing to another
without the ability to settle or be satisfied with any
particular pursuit. I look at it differently. Because
I have tried this and that, I believe I can recognize
and appreciate a certain value in endeavors or in
people that others might overlook. From that vantage
point, I can actually save time and energy in the long
run. I am in reality a happy wanderer.*

*Ah, if only that were the end of the situation. Wandering
has its drawbacks. Society does not approve of
wanderers. The connotation of wandering seems to
represent a shiftless behavior with no serious plans or
prospects. So, to be a happy wanderer one must cover
it up. You have to pretend to have a life design with goals
that represent permanence. If that does not succeed, you
are branded as a radical, a misfit, a nondoer with deviant
behavior. It is a label that invites struggle, controversy,
and opposition. It can cause a substantial infringement
on happiness. But, why can't life be a tune on a music
box? Why have tunes? Why have music boxes?*

Polite applause abated before Connor offered his comments. "I guess I should change the name of this course to Depression 101. It would have been nice to have something light-hearted to offset the doom and gloom. Maybe I have over-emphasized the struggle and frustration of writing. Yet, if the driving force is a display of negativism then you join those ranks. The somber depths do furnish caverns on thought to explore, more so than maybe happiness and exuberance towards life. Please be careful that it does not spill into your everyday experiences and feelings. This is the time of your lives that it is far better to enjoy the sunshine than to lurk in the shadows."

*Books aren't written, they're rewritten.
Including your own. It is one of the hardest
things to accept, especially after the rewrite
hasn't quite done it.*

Michael Crichton

*The difference between fiction and reality?
Fiction has to make sense.*

Tom Clancy

***

TWENTY-ONE

After he arrived at the University it started to snow. The snow kept getting heavier and when a fierce northwest wind whipped up blizzard conditions set in.

There was a warm and friendly telephone message from Kelly. She had hoped he had a good Thanksgiving break, and then talked about rereading one of his books and offered some germane comments. Kelly had shifted to a different tact about Connor while she was home with the family. She toned down romantic stories about them as a couple and realized that it might be more realistic and productive at this juncture to concentrate efforts at establishing a close friendship. He was receptive to that kind of overture, and he appreciated her interest and intelligence and sensed a genuine attention. He called her before his nightly call to Celia to check if she had enough provisions to get through the storm. He mentioned that when the weather was more hospitable he would like to accompany her on some walks with the dog.

Classes were cancelled the next day because of the severe weather conditions. This afforded him the opportunity to catch up on grading papers, working on his own book, and starting to read Celia's books. Her writing style was fluid and whimsical. It was readily apparent why her books were so popular. Bailey was an intriguing and entertaining character.

Rather than letting the freshmen read, he gave them a pop quiz on the outside readings and the moans and groans greeted that announcement. The story assignment was not collected as he told them to hold on to them until he returned from the book conference. The additional assignment was given of writing an uplifting story. He certainly did not want any more depressing prose. It was important that they feel good about the stories they wrote. If any would eventually become a serious writer, there would be ample opportunity to agonize over plots and the misfortunes of characters. There would be a high degree of frustration and debilitating behavior. That was a given.

The New York City book conference was in full swing when he arrived there. The panel he was to be on was scheduled for the afternoon of the second day. Except for going out for dinner, he spent the time in the hotel room preparing for the fifteen-minute presentation he was to give. Before going to sleep, he telephoned Celia and the long conversation was as usual warm and stimulating.

He was several minutes into his talk when he focused on a figure in the audience about halfway back. It was Dorie. The impact was absorbed by a momentary pause in his speaking. It was a good thing he had the notes before him or his train of thought would have been sidetracked. There is no way to fully prepare for the many surprises that emerge in life.

At the end of the panel's session he approached her as the audience was filing out. She stood and smiled. She was still pretty and fetching. The black hair was longer and hung straight down with an alluring sheen highlighted by the overhead lights. The face was the picture of the Dorie of her youth, clear and not a wrinkle to mar the skin. The slim body was encased in a form-fitting black pants suit with a white turtleneck sweater. She hugged him earnestly and pressed that all too familiar body against him.

When she broke loose, her broad smile was unchanged. A past suddenly became his present. "Connor," her voice soft and tinged with emotion, "you look so good. You have changed little, and your talk was captivating."

He fumbled for the words, and they seemed so dumb. "What are you doing here?"

"I still write poetry. I have not had the success you have had, and I might add a success well deserved. I came for the poetry session tomorrow morning but when I saw you listed in the program, I could not stay away."

It was not easy to formulate his thoughts. "It has been a long time." He wondered if that was the most appropriate way to say it.

Her long eyelashes accentuated the gaze as she shifted it to the floor. "A long time but in many ways it is like yesterday. I have never stopped thinking about you and remembering the times we had together."

They went out to the foyer and sat on a bench off from the crowd. He noticed a slight trembling of her fingers. He was sure his own voice was shaking. "Why did you let it go?"

Her voice was low and almost drowned out by the background noise. "I didn't, willingly. You were always the strong one. My personal weakness was no match for the pressure from my father. That was a mistake I should have recognized from the beginning. After we moved to New Jersey I went to a community college and got my degree. He persistently told me to forget you and that my place, no my duty, was to be with a Jewish boy. We joined a synagogue and he must have arranged for every eligible man in the congregation to date me. Primarily to get him off my back I married one of them. Seven months later I divorced him, at long last coming to my senses. Yet, I was ashamed and maybe even too obstinate to contact you. I messed up my life, and I did not want to infringe on yours. I got my own apartment here in the city near where we used to live, found a job, and lost myself in my poetry and memories. I followed your career. I have read each of your books many times, seeing in them the young and clever man I had known. I like to think I saw what many others might have missed. I even saw some of me along the way, and frankly you graced me with kind qualities I really do not have."

He reached for her hand and it was as natural as each breath that he took. "One thing has not changed. You are still unnecessarily hard on yourself."

As if she did not want to address that statement, believing in her heart it was a punishment to bear, she changed the subject. "How are your parents?"

Thinking it best not to press the issue, he fell into the conversation shift. "They are well. They are in a retirement home in North Carolina and are content. I saw them over Thanksgiving."

"I am not sure they approved of me, but they were certainly more tolerant than my father was about you."

"You were the only girl I ever brought home to meet them, and they grew to respect you as they knew how much you meant to me."

"I have often wished I could turn the clock back. Now that I am with you, I wonder if it is truly possible to capture the past."

He hesitated before speaking, a bevy of emotions pulling him in various directions. "I believe it is best to leave the past alone. If memories are disturbed they may lose their luster."

She stroked his arm through the sports jacket he was wearing. "How can you be so sure of that?"

"I have recently met a wonderful woman who has captivated me just as you did in high school. My absorption is total. Teaching and writing have filled every crevice of my being. Dorie, it is wonderful to see you again and I am so glad you are still a poet. I often thought about where you might be and what you were doing. It is comforting to know you are alright."

Dorie tried to hold back the tears but they came anyway. It was a great risk to come to the Conference with the expectation of seeing him and hoping to erase the intervening years. She was convinced that what they had was very special and that could and should make it feasible to fulfill that promise. She looked deeply into his eyes and spoke between the sobs. "I am not alright. I fully realize that I need and want you in my life again. If this be a test between the old and the new, I'll take my chances. I know in my heart what we were is what we can be."

He softened with her crying. "We are too old for tests, Dorie. But, let's stay in touch. Give me your address. I have a shoebox full of your poems that I want to return to you."

She wrote out the address, the tears still rolling down her cheeks. "It is in the old neighborhood. Since you are not leaving until tomorrow, for old time's sake, please come over for dinner tonight. I promise I will not put any pressure on you."

A reluctance nagged at him and he knew far too well that he should not accept such a temptation. "O.K." He shrugged off the weakness in his character.

The small apartment was simply and tastefully decorated. That had always been an admirable attribute of her personality. She shied away from the glossy and ornate. Pleasures emanated from ordinary and uncomplicated touches and experiences. The meal was a further reflection of such a stance. A salad was followed by a vegetable omelet and then a dish of ice cream for dessert. The wine was a plain California Merlot.

He helped her clean up and they sat on the sofa finishing the wine. The sweater and slacks she wore graced a body that he guessed had retained the youthful fitness she had prided herself on. Her movements and voice were as animated as they used to be. "These twelve years have treated you well. You have a handsome maturity that I had guessed you would have."

"Ah, and the years for you have merely refined perfection."

Her smile was captivating. "An author's comments, for sure."

"Writers see the world differently or as it is. I am not sure there is a distinction."

She took a sip of wine. "I promised I would not pressure you. Yet, being with you has erased the time we have been apart. I have all of the old feelings, even stronger. I would like nothing better than for us to be together."

He placed his glass on the coffee table, careful to use the coaster. "I will be as honest as I can. I have missed you and missed what we had, but I know that is in the past and I have entered a new present with a future admittedly not fully defined and yet promising." A pause accentuated his uncertainty as he tried to take the noble course. "The past is best left in the past."

"Kiss me and then say all that again and I will believe you."

"Let me put it another way. Seeing you today is a shock and one that I was ill prepared to handle. Sure, some of the good memories flow in, and I am a bit confused about it. I need to return to the University to sort things out. Kissing you, as pleasant as the thought might be, would not help."

There was no kiss, although they hugged when he left. He sensed an urgency in the pressure of her body against his, and found that tantalizing. At the hotel, he called Celia shielding any troublesome reactions.

It was a restless night for a mind in overdrive. He tried to keep Celia's image sharp, although visions of Dorie as she was today as well as in the collage of memories of the past infringed on the scene. How would all of this be resolved? He had not the slightest clue.

> Oh, how cruelly sweet are the echoes that
> start when Memory plays an old tune on
> the heart!

Elisa Cook

Daniel Hill Zafren

*Only in one's imagination does every truth
find an effective and undeniable existence.
Imagination, not inventions is the supreme
master of art as of life.*

Joseph Conrad

***

TWENTY-TWO

Dorie lingered on the sofa long after Connor had left. She was not tired. In fact, she felt exhilarated as those wonderful sensations she had long since pushed into the recesses of her mind flooded in. She was as sure now as she was back then that Connor was the true love of her life. Back in high school, so fervently believing they would spend their entire lives together, she must have scribbled Dorie Chase thousands of times in her school notebooks.

The resentment towards her father had built up over the years, and she blamed him for altering what she believed was her destiny. That negative outlook had spread to all things Jewish, and she avoided contact with Jewish people when she could.

The only positive that emerged was that it added a thrust of energy and purpose to her poetry. From what used to be timid and a gentle flow of words and ideas, some of the intensity of her creations now shook her to the core. That kind of forcefulness would be channeled to relentlessly pursue Connor. She was that sure of herself and her feelings for him.

Before she went to bed, she opened her laptop and sent Connor an e-mail message at the address he had given her.

My Dearest Connor:

I already feel the pain of your absence as I have suffered through the long period deprived of your love and companionship. Being with you has only sharpened my belief that we are made for one another. Reviewing our early relationship, I just know that you will reach the same conclusion.

No doubt, you feel some anger and disappointment in me for turning away from what we had. I cannot deny that such feelings would be natural. I fully realize what I gave up and, my darling, I will strive every day of my life to make it up to you.

*My feelings and promises are bound in what I do best –
a poem especially for you, a rhyming one since I assume*

you still do not care for free verse.

THE INVITING FLAME OF LOVE

Love is a fire that cannot be extinguished,
It can be a robust blaze or appear to have died;
Love can be frantic or refined and distinguished,
Its genuine presence cannot and should not be denied.

So, my love, let this fire warm your spirit,
Let it guide, protect, and nourish;
A special love has a fire of particular merit,
Do not turn from it so that it may flourish!

Dorie closed the laptop after sending the message. Her heart was full and her mind racing ahead with the possibility of the full realization of her dreams. Dorie Chase appeared so close she was sure all she had to do was to reach out and grab it.

It's none of their business that you have to learn to write. Let them think you were born that way.

Ernest Hemingway

Whatever an author puts between the two covers of his book is public property; whatever of himself he does not put there is his private property, as much as if he had never written a word.

Mary Abigail Dodge

TWENTY-THREE

The first freshman to read one of his stories was Henry Farrell. He chose not to read the uplifting story he had written because he was more inspired by the story of anguish that had proven to be an emotional trial.

THE LIFE OF A SECRET

*Is a secret forever? Or, once the person whose
secret it was dies, does that release the need
or reason for secrecy?*

*Robert Newall only knew the heavy burden of
keeping Albert Hinert's secret for many years.
It had always puzzled him that he remembered
that secret in such great detail. Why couldn't
he have forgotten it with the many things he no
longer could recall? The two men had never
mentioned it or discussed it after that fateful
day that Albert had unleashed those powerful
events sworn to be hidden. Since such was
part of who Albert was, did his widow and
children have a right to know? Would it be
fair if Albert could not answer the questions
that would certainly arise about it or to further
explain it? After all, its nature was such
that there might be more than one interpretation
of the facts. In fact, Robert had on more than
one occasion wanted to question Albert about
the specifics. Believing that this might further
complicate his involvement in the secret, he
had refrained from doing so.*

*So, what momentous happening had affected the
life of Albert and then fell upon Robert? It cannot
be divulged. Robert swore never to reveal it.*

The class applause was genuine. Connor shook his head, second-guessing himself that perhaps writers, especially new ones, would rather write about the misery that people wallow in than the bright and touching moments that adheres people to people. "Henry, that was thought-provoking. I liked the opening and closing, even though it would probably not satisfy the curious reader who would like to know what must be a powerful secret. I know your concentration was on the emotions of an innocent person dragged into the situation."

Chagrined once again that she was not first to read, Abigail Torrence resigned herself to be second. The professor was placing an obstacle in front of her constant desire to be first, although she would not let it derail her.

MEMORY FLASHES

We've all heard of hot flashes. A memory flash is when an older person suddenly remembers this or that from the past, invariably forgotten soon after the recall.

It was her favorite time of the day. The retirement home served tea at three o'clock, and Fedora Heina would then go with her friends on the broad expanse back porch where the rockers were lined up. Rocking gently, most of them would doze off but not Fedora. A ninety-year-old woman did not have too many clear thinking times, and the afternoon ritual somehow often provided a stimulus to recall events long forgotten, a memory flash.

There had to be many memories for a remarkable woman. When she graduated from law school sixty-five years ago, she had been the only female in the school. It mattered not that the wall street law firm that hired her was more anxious to capitalize on the oddity of having a woman lawyer there. She had demanded and received a very high salary and many other benefits. They got their money's worth as she

116

brought in many female clients the firm would
not otherwise have had.

Being smart was not her only asset. She was
drop-dead beautiful. Every law student fell over
himself to impress her. At the law firm, even
the married partners behaved like high school
boys in her presence. As she aged, the good looks
faded and she easily relied more and more on
her intelligence. Along with that came a stubborn
independence. She never married and had no
children. She often wondered what it would
have been like to have children, and it saddened
her when the children of other residents came to
visit. She had a career and when that was
over, the emptiness took over.

So, it was in these memory flashes that she had
numerous lovers and successes, and there were
incidents that probably never happened or took
on exaggerated form. The fragility of life
encompasses every moment and it is accentuated
by the time it is over. If she did have children,
that would be the reasoning she would pass on
to them. A memory flash can be tinged with
the wisdom of the ages, the now wisdom of
the aged.

Abigail smiled at the student applause. Connor joined in. "Abigail, evidently everybody thought that was awfully good. I liked the opening and closing, and you made the character quite real. You show great promise, young lady."

Next on the firing line was Deborah Barnes. She showed some hesitation in volunteering after that well received effort by Abigail, but she believed in her own ability and that would prevail.

HOPE, UNLIMITED

What's in a name? Her parents had named
her Hope believing it would cast a positive

*aura on all of their lives. It seemed to work.
The growing years were happy ones, and there
were many proud accomplishments as she
emerged into adulthood.*

*Her dream was to have her own business.
It was a given that the name of the business
would be Hope, Unlimited. Exactly, what
that business would be was elusive. It took
major capital to start and run a business.
She was stymied by the chicken and egg
puzzle. Do you raise the money first and
then develop the business idea, or do you
need the idea first? The people she talked
to were split on this, although most agreed
it would probably be easier to raise money
if the concept was present and then
persuasive.*

*It was then that Hope met Faith.
They became instant friends and
Faith liked the idea of going into
business together. Hope and Faith,
Unlimited had a nice ring to it.
With a name like that, how could any
business fail?*

*The problem overwhelmed them.
They could neither raise a sufficient
amount of money or come up with a
novel business concept. Faith gave up
Hope. Hope gave up Faith.*

The sustained applause was noted by Connor. "Clever story, Deborah. Evidently, everyone liked it. All of you are making good progress. Keep up the good work."

The writer's head is mobbed
with characters, images, and
language, making the creative
process something like
eavesdropping at a party for
which you've had the fun of
drawing up the guest list.

Hilma Wolitzer

Better put a strong fence 'round
the top of the cliff
Than an ambulance down in the
valley.

Joseph Malines

***

TWENTY-FOUR

Inspiration and steady intentions do not always produce results. Celia was having a difficult time writing. Fresh thoughts were needed before the words could appear. It was too chilly outside, so she was lounging at the kitchen table while all she could think about was Connor. She was perceptive enough to know that he was more reserved then he had been. She refused to place a negative connotation on it. Knowing better than most, people at times needed to step back before they can proceed forwards.

She looked for Sherlock so they could go over to Bee's house. She found him sprawled out on her bed draped over Connor's books. It was a game of pretense that she had his books on her bed. By having the books there it was almost as if he was there too. Sherlock had his paws over the books as if he was clutching at them. It sure made a cute picture. Celia would mention just an image to Connor for consideration as a front cover for the book he was writing. Such a cover would be symbolic as well as appealing. Books are authors' pet peeves.

Sipping coffee and nibbling on the oatmeal raisin cookies Bee had made for the children's lunch boxes, the friends drew great comfort from this daily ritual. Support comes in many guises. It can be in a word, a hug, or merely in a presence. Cee blurted out, "I cannot concentrate on writing."

Bee covered her hand with her own. "Little wonder. An uncomplicated life suddenly has new developments. If it were me, I would be unable to paint."

"You always say just the right things. I am blessed to have you."

"I savor all of our times together. Our feelings are so much alike I often think we are one and the same person. So, what do you think this Connor fella is planning?"

Celia leaned backwards trying to adjust to an unwelcome weariness that seeped into her body. "I don't think he is planning anything. He is a writer. He is probably letting all of the events and sensations settle in as if he were to write a story about it. He has a cool head and will not take action until he is ready. I am not too concerned."

"You are the cool one. I may have to start biting my nails and take up smoking."

"If you do you may have trouble holding a brush, and the last thing you want is for a canvas to smell from cigarette smoke."

"Thanks for pointing that out. Maybe I'll just pig out on these cookies."

"That, dear friend, I can join you in."

"He is still coming for Christmas, isn't he?? The children and I bought him a present. It is under the tree."

"Yes, he talks about it each time we speak."

"That's encouraging. If he doesn't come I'll return the present and stomp on him whenever he does show up."

"That'll put the fear in him for sure. You had better find a different form of annoyance than stomping. There is not a violent bone in your body."

"I would do anything to protect you and to see that you get what is just."

"Likewise."

"I know that, dear heart."

They hugged before Bee headed out for the studio. Cee and Sherlock walked slowly back to the house. Just thinking about Connor spread a warmth through her system. "He must know that no one is going to love him as I do," she thought firmly to herself.

Back at the house, she was still unable to concentrate on Bailey's latest involvement. She tried again after lunch, with no success. She cleaned the house and did some ironing. Putting some final touches on the decorations for the Christmas tree, she liked how it looked and enjoyed the pungent pine smell from the fresh tree. It was all festive to match Connor's soon to be arrival.

Their telephone conversation that evening was as usual fulfilling. She was sure of him and herself. A smile appeared as this confidence produced the promise of what was meant to be and it would transport her to a place that until recently she believed would never be.

Of course, the writer cannot always burn with
a hard gemlike flame or a white heat, but it
should be possible to be a chubby hot water
bottle, rendering maximum attentiveness in
the most enterprising sentences.

Paul West

To burn always with this hard, gemlike flame,
to maintain this ecstasy, is success in life.

Walter Pater

122

Daniel Hill Zafren

Have you had a kindness shown?
Pass it on. . . .

Hold thy lighted lamp on high,
Be a star in someone's sky.

Harry Burton

***

TWENTY-FIVE

Connor exchanged email messages daily with Dorie, each one taking on longer expositions of who they were then and who they are now. Each evening, the telephone conversation with Celia was most enjoyable, particularly when they talked about writing. He wondered how long he could hold off deciding which love interest was the most significant. It would be an easy alternative to bypass both Celia and Dorie and take up with Kelly. Every man should have this kind of dilemma

That Saturday morning was warm for the time of year and Connor joined Kelly for a walk with Gildersleeve. She was a good listener, and each of her animated reactions was appropriate and appreciated. Kelly was attractive and intellectually challenging. Her interest in him seemed quite genuine.

Kelly was heartened by Connor's overture to participate in the walk with Gil. The way she figured it, the more time they spent together he might more easily realize that she was the kind of woman he needed to be with. She had already decided that about him, and a mutuality of feelings and expectations would produce a worthwhile end.

After the walk, they went to Kelly's house for coffee and a slice of the walnut pound cake she had made the night before. She loved to bake not only for its creative element but also for its sharp contrast from her academic activity. It sure did please her when Connor asked for a second piece.

"I could use another walk after eating this cake," he said jokingly. "Each time I think you can't possibly improve on the last masterpiece, you surpass that standard."

"I am glad you are that attentive. We can walk anytime you wish. I have said before, if I didn't get much exercise I would be a blimp eating my efforts. I sure do envy those folks who can eat all they want to and not gain any weight."

"There's no justice in the world."

"That's a fact."

"How is your text coming along?"

"Fairly well. I use feedback from my students to stimulate topics and questions."

"I have the same approach for my book. The student writings prompt me to analyze and discuss nuances of literary undertakings. They seem to enjoy writing, and it sure shows in their stories. Some of them show great promise. I can lead the way, but only they can decide to stick with it."

"It can be a great responsibility to inspire others."

"Absolutely, and I do not take it lightly. Hardships seem to be more numerous than rewards, and that can be a bitter pill to swallow."

Kelly was careful to phrase her words. "In a way you also inspire me. If I know you will be sharing some of my baked goods, I proceed easily. Knowing you are a few doors away writing, then my text efforts are less difficult. I believe strongly that people need other people to do their best."

"I believe that as well. There are many authors, however, who shun other people and are convinced that their best work can only be produced in isolation."

"That is a self-imposed deprivation. For my point-of-view, it limits perspective."

"I suppose it is just a case of each person loving his own misery best."

"And that is how they usually turn out – miserable."

Over the next hour, they talked of many things. It was pleasant, and the atmosphere was eased by bursts of laughter. She had a keen sense of humor, and he especially enjoyed her play on words. That was sure to hold the attention of a writer. Before he put his coat on, they hugged. He was well aware of her full soft body as she pressed close to him. Ah, the mystery of the subtle attraction of the here and now.

Later that day when he savored the extra piece of cake she had sent home with him, he had to rethink the dilemma as being one that any man would like. Or, perhaps, he was not just any man. He sensed that there might be a whole heap of trouble before he fixed on the direction of true happiness.

Some books are undeservedly forgotten;
none are undeservedly remembered.

W.H, Auden

Let me live, love and say it well in good sentences.

Sylvia Plath

To know is nothing at all; to imagine is everything.

Anatole France

TWENTY-SIX

The entire workshop class was anxious to read their stories. Connor scanned the sea of raised hands, settling on Ken Trollop. He stood and then read slowly from the sheets of paper clutched firmly in his hands.

A GOOD NEIGHBOR

I am not sure exactly when it happened, but I knew why it had to happen. My wife and I and our two small children lived in one of those cookie-cutter communities filled with young families. My wife grew increasingly bitter and resentful of me, the children and the community. She never wanted children and had given up a career in the world of fashion at my urging for a family. She was bored with the community and could not tolerate the inane conversation with other mothers about children and routine household activities. My guilt increased, and our relationship deteriorated.

Next door, there was also a young man and woman with two small children. However, it was the husband who was bitter. He was confined to a wheelchair from a hunting accident. His discontent drove a wedge in the marriage.

After the children were in bed, my neighbor wife and I had the same routine of going out for a jog around the neighborhood. Eventually, we started jogging together. Conversation became more consoling and intimate, and a mutual need for some tenderness led to a romantic involvement. At the end of the jog, under the cover of darkness, we would go behind the garage to her house. No windows faced that space, and a row of trees behind

*the houses provided ample secrecy. For a brief time
we would hold one another with welcome gentle
affection. It soothed the harsh reality and gave us
the impetus to tolerate an unhappy home life.*

*There were inevitable discussions of carrying the
relationship further and perhaps running away
together. Because of the tender age of the children
and our loyalty to them, we decided to stick with
our bleak prospects. Our moments of escape would
have to suffice, although they became more urgent.
The bond between us strengthened. Every option
was explored without practical resolution. It
seemed as if we had reached an impasse.*

*As if preordained, a series of events brought a
solution. My wife left me, abandoning the
children and suburbia. My neighbor's husband,
after a serious bout of depression, committed suicide.
After these events settled down, and my divorce was
final, my neighbor and I married and merged our
two families. As if the symbolism was perpetual,
we often met behind the garage for an embrace.*

Ken acknowledged the applause with a nod of his head as he sat down. Connor waited a moment before he offered his comments. "Ken, there certainly was a great deal crammed into this story. The facts were recited as your journalistic background trained you. There was, however, scant delving into the characters and you merely brushed the surface of their emotions. There is ample material there for a book. A short story is a snippet of an event, but it can be weak if the total picture needs to be exposed. Here, you posed four complex personalities without detailing their thoughts and explaining sufficiently the reasoning behind major actions. Even reactions by the children would have lent a certain depth to the situation. Advice for all of you after you write is to step back and ask yourself if it has done the job. There are instances when fewer characters and developments can produce a more endearing and enduring story. As with so many other facets of life, more does not always mean better."

The next student to read was Gwen Jenner. Before she spoke, there was a brief hesitation. Connor guessed that either she was not totally sure of herself or she was using that as an attention getting device.

HALF A GLASS

The glass stood alone on the table
      Half its contents consumed,
To speak if it was able
      Half full or half empty – can it be presumed?
The story-teller can reveal the scene,
The listener must interpret the dream.

Without a doubt, it takes effort to be optimistic or
pessimistic. Is the effort equal? Does the
situation dictate the extent of the effort? What
if the person has an inclination to be one way or
the other? What about the theory that if you are
optimistic you are bound to have more disappointments
while if pessimistic there might be more pleasant
surprises?

From an early age, Chloe Harbinger was confused
about where she stood on the optimism-pessimism
issue. She really wanted to be a little of each to
be as resilient as possible. That was difficult, so
she did the next best thing, she was neither. The
only problem with that was that if neither, she in fact
was pessimistic. If you are not hopeful or believe the
best in events and people, you are in reality not hopeful
at all and think little of things and people. You can call
yourself realistic but at the end of the day you are only
fooling yourself.

All of this came to a head when Chloe was to go for
an interview for the job of her dreams. It was two weeks
away and she was a nervous wreck. If she did not get this
job, what would become of her? That sure was pessimistic
enough but how do you rationalize away something that
is so vital to your being? She wanted to be upbeat and
concentrate on the thought of prevailing over the other

qualified candidates. It might be important to impart
confidence at the interview. Yet, it was impossible to
sustain that thought. That was a form of pessimism in
itself.

By the time the interview was held, Chloe was consumed
by the negative possibilities. It detracted from her demeanor
and she was sure she did not do her best. That was
confirmed when another was selected.

She telephoned her mother with the bad news. "Mom,
I did not get the job."

"Don't worry, dear. It just means something better will
come along. You are young, bright, and talented. The
world is your oyster."

"I'm not so sure of that."
"I am. You are my daughter, and I can see it all as
plain as day."

Her mother always made her feel better. Her mother was
an eternal optimist. Chloe could only hope that such a trait
proved to be hereditary.

Robust applause greeted Gwen's finish. The students liked it and Connor was taken with it as an able piece of writing. "Gwen, you certainly held my interest and I could not guess where you were going with it. Good job. It set forth a valuable lesson of life while being engrossing. That is successful writing. That we can be optimistic about. I also liked the introductory verse. That is a nice touch."

Gordy Anterwick was next. Connor was hoping as was the student's bent that the story would be humorous. That would be refreshing.

A RABBIT'S FOOT

"Are you superstitious?" My friend's question forced me
to take a good look at myself.

"Stupiditious?"

"No, superstitious. For example, do you believe a rabbit's foot brings good luck?"

"Believe me, I wouldn't even think of eating a rabbit, so I certainly am not going to be carrying around its foot."

"Would you walk under a ladder? Shudder if a black cat runs in front of you?"

I thought for a moment. "Life is hard enough. Why would I want to complicate it further by having to raise artificial choices?"

"Then, how do you explain society's consideration of such things? Some buildings do not have a thirteenth floor."

"There is no end to what commercialism will or will not do to attract or not offend folks. That is stupiditious."

Later, when I was alone, I realized that most of us have some habits that could easily be labeled as superstitious. When I was young, I used to chew hard foods on the left side of my mouth and soft foods on the right side. When I would meet an attractive girl that I wanted to date, I would recite this little ditty before asking her out – "She has just my kind of body and face, just right for my kind of embrace." At one point, I was convinced my amorous plights were totally dependent on that ritual. Now, I know better. Or, at least I think I know better. Yet, I probably should not analyze things too closely. If I did, I might have to open the glove compartment of my car and find another place to put the rabbit's foot.

The hardy applause was well deserved. It was a light-hearted story, and it was a breath of fresh air. Stories with a touch of humor can be effective and highly entertaining. Connor used that theme to close out the session and to emphasize once again that writing can be as expansive as thinking.

Writing is a socially acceptable form of schizophrenia.

E. L. Doctorow

*The reason that fiction is more interesting than
any other form of literature, to those who
really like to study people, is that in fiction the
author can really tell the truth without
humiliating himself.*

Eleanor Roosevelt

*To be what we are, and to become what we are capable
of becoming, is the only end of life.*

Robert Louis Stevenson

TWENTY-SEVEN

The benefit of a short Christmas shopping list is that it does not take long to collect the goodies. For Kelly, it was a set of a matching hat, scarf, and mittens that he thought she could use on her dog walks. For Dorie, even though she did not celebrate Christmas, since he had given her presents at the holiday when they were together that he had called love gifts, he had found a book of poems by unknown poets. He just knew she would like it. For his parents, it was a houseplant. He had noticed such were allowed where they were. As a boy, he remembered the many plants they tended to on the wide windowsills, another attribute of those old windows. For Becca and her family, a specially packaged selection of pure fruit preserves. By chance, he had found the perfect gift for Celia when he ducked into the antique shop in town. It was an old musical trinket box with a painting of a Yorkshire terrier on the lid.

There had been additional walks with Kelly and Gildersleeve, and he gave her the gift the day before she was to leave for home. He was to leave two days later for New York for three days and then on to Celia and to visit his parents. Kelly gave him a blueberry loaf straight from the oven.

Connor did not like to lie, but he did not tell Celia about Dorie and he said he had to do some research for a few days in New York. It was not actually a lie as he convinced himself that he needed to do research to make sure there was nothing to pursue with Dorie. If there turned out to be something there, he would tell Celia. If not, then he would have spared her of any hurt and anxiety. Kelly was not an actual consideration at this point but was more of an alternative if the course of events led to the need for an alternative. A writer can rationalize with the best of them, except perhaps for a politician.

Even with the slight delay, Cee was happily looking forward to the nearly two weeks that Connor would be with her. She took extra care decorating the house, even using some Christmas items she had not put out for years. She was sure it would be a wonderful Christmas. There would be the usual warm and inviting times with Becca and her family all enhanced by her man sharing the memories.

Dorie was more nervous than she thought she would be waiting for him. The exchanged messages while probing were noncommittal and she knew that Connor had doubts about her. She was quite certain of her expectations. He had said he would stay for a day or maybe three days depending on how things went. Her hope was that he stay long and return often, and she had to make sure that would be the way it turned out. She had much to make up for and was prepared not to let this opportunity slip by.

She had a pasta dinner waiting for him. After a firm embrace, they ate while engaging in polite conversation. After cleaning up from the meal, they sat on the sofa. She gushed with delight opening up the book of poets. She gave him his present. "This is just part of my love gift to you."

He opened the package to find a framed photograph of them that a stranger had taken on one of their outings to the Union Square bookstores. He thought to himself that she had retained all of that youthful beauty. "Thank you. Those were wonderful times."

She grasped his hand. "There can be many more wonderful times ahead to share. At a time when I knew I loved you, I did not know much about love itself. Now, that love which has always been with me has emerged stronger and more purposeful. I understand what we had, a relationship that few are fortunate enough to have. Can you ever forgive me for not fully recognizing that and protecting it and perpetuating it?"

"There is nothing to forgive you for. It was a special time but we were young and foolish in so many ways. Maturity can bring regrets, but we cannot judge what we were then unless we can see who we are now. You may be equating guilt with love."

"No, I am not," she spoke forcefully tears forming at the corners of her eyes. "I am more sure of this than anything else. I will prove it to you over the days we have together. The only thing I ask of you is to give me this chance and to be patient with me."

They kissed before he left for the hotel for the night. It was a tender kiss, pleasant to the senses and reminiscent of an earlier time. Can time actually stand still for some purposes?

At the hotel, he telephoned Celia and it was apparent how excited she was with the near prospect of his visit. He hoped he would not disappoint her.

The next day, they visited some of the used bookstores that still remained from those earlier trips. Lunch at a delicatessen kindled some former moments. They saw an old movie at a repertory theater. Back at her apartment, Dorie made dinner and then they lounged on the sofa after a tiring but satisfying day. They held hands, fingers intertwined comfortably. An ardent kiss and hug followed capturing for the moment old sensations. She wanted him to spend the night with her but he was not prepared to do that. Dorie did not pressure him, confident that she was winning him over gradually. Even a slow victory can be most sweet.

The next morning, they met for breakfast at one of their old haunts, The Hot Shoppe. The place was still the same, and that in itself was amazing when everything seemed to change without reason. He had often commented in general that nothing stays the same. They lingered over a third cup of coffee, talking about writing and about poetry. There were candid expressions about the life around and beyond them. Dorie read aloud a poem she had especially liked from the volume he had given her.

They discussed at length the emotions of the poet and her message. Friends in high school had described them as deep people. They had readily accepted that description, and they still were like that. Each had little satisfaction with literature and life unless analysis and discussion delved into the particular obvious elements and the hidden subtleties. It is a form of restlessness that can only be quieted by active and probing minds. This had not changed.

They went to The Museum of Natural History and then walked through Central Park. They skipped lunch because of the bountiful breakfast they had consumed.

At the apartment as he watched her working in the kitchen on a meal for them, he found it troubling that his main thought was to lead her to the bedroom and to make love to her. Her overt actions had continually tempted him in that direction. She teased him as she used to do believing his resistance to her charms was limited. Connor had been content with himself as a writer. He would not be proud of himself as a man.

When he left for Celia's house, Dorie wept as she clutched at him. She had taken in all the descriptions about Celia and could not deny she was jealous. Yet, it was more than that. Letting him leave now was a symbol of her giving him up as she had done once before. All she could do was to declare her fervent love for him and to make sure he knew her kisses and hugs were in earnest. Her comfort was to believe he would not ignore what was rediscovered. She would be here for him. She made sure he knew that.

> *Better to write for yourself and have no*
> *public, than to write for the public and*
> *have no self.*

> Cyril Connally

> *How do I know what I think until I see*
> *what I say?*

> E. M. Forster

> *I am bigger than anything that can happen*
> *to me. All these things, sorrow, misfortune,*
> *and suffering, are outside my door. I am*
> *in the house and I have the key.*

> Charles Fletcher Lummis

***

TWENTY-EIGHT

It was during the first night when they were making love that Celia sensed something was troubling him. He was hesitant, ever so slightly, that one who was not so much in love might not have noticed. He assured her all was well, and he had already decided not to tell her about Dorie until after Christmas day. He had highly praised her for the festive decorations in the house, and he wanted the first few days to be calm and relaxed. He would keep his internal upheaval to himself. He was sure he loved Celia, but he could not deny there were strong feelings towards Dorie and an almost uncontrollable impulse pulling him in her direction.

What he could not predict or control was a rising and overbearing desire to work on his book. It had been a struggle with a sentence or paragraph here and there with frustration becoming increasingly apparent. On the next day he explained this driving force to Celia, perhaps only another author could understand and sympathize with such a plight. She left him alone to work and went to Bee's house with Sherlock.

"So, where is he?" Bee hugged her as she looked past her down the walk.

"He is writing. A creative tidal wave has swept him away."

"I'd rather it be a marital wave."

"All in good time, dear friend. As both a writer and one who loves him, I cannot and will not squelch a creative urge. After all, it could easily be the other way around."

"I have those moments when the need to paint obscures nearly everything. Yet, I cannot exclude those I love."

"Love can foster obsessions of all sorts."

"Only a writer can understand and believe that."

"And a writer's best friend should abide by assurances, even the imaginary ones."

Bee hugged her again. "I hope you know what you are doing. Remember we are not only friends, we are the concocted concept of fris, friends without end."

"Who can be sure what they do all of the time? I am sure of our fris, and that has sustained me and will always do so even down pathways which may appear dark."

Becca thought to herself, "Maybe killing him would be too good for him."

The tale for Connor's book had taken shape. An aspiring writer was struggling with the writing. A lawyer friend advised him not to use real names or to follow too precisely the actual stories of real people. All of this becomes agonizingly fuzzy in the writer's mind. An overwhelming compulsion forces him to ignore the advice and to flounder haphazardly in the realm between fact and fiction. If the unlikely result were that a real person would identify with the character in the book with the prospect of a potential lawsuit, surely that person would know that he had no malice in mind and would not heed the advice of others. The book was essentially a dual struggle for the writer between conscience and societal dictates. Inner and outer turmoil takes its toll on both the author and the character he creates.

In the quiet of the house, Connor looked beyond the pages and the passages. He was astute enough to know that just such a personal conflict involved his own life. Monumental consequences were at risk for the protagonist in the book as well as for himself. Perhaps both were in situations that could not be controlled.

They exchanged presents just before they went to Becca's house for Christmas dinner. Celia was elated by the music box, and she hugged Connor with warm affection. Her present to him was a sleek leather portfolio designed for sorting and storing loose papers. It would suit him well in his writing pursuits and for taking notes to the conferences. It was a thoughtful gift and most appreciated. It would always be with him as she wished it to be.

The meal was a feast that Becca went all out to make special. The children were excited with their gifts, and the family gave Connor a sterling silver pen. It was a day filled with laughter and sentimental thoughts. Bee put aside any doubts she had about Connor for the moment sensing that Cee was happy and relaxed.

The day after Christmas, Connor took Celia to meet his parents. They had lunch together at the home before the folks took the houseplant back to their lodging. The conversation had been flowing, and the parents accepted Celia as a serious choice by their son. His mother could tell that Celia was older than Connor, and she tried to shake that concept off although an old-fashioned person has some difficulty adapting to current social acceptances. His father wondered why his son did not choose a prettier woman, and he still remembered the beautiful Dorie that Connor had brought home. However, they were impressed by Celia's outgoing personality, and it was obvious that she had strong amorous feelings toward Connor. They appreciated her warm hug as they left.

On the drive back, Celia asked a bit too hastily, "Do you think they liked me?"

"Who wouldn't?"

"A set of parents who see a woman trying to steal their son away."

"They are not that way. I have only brought one girl ever to meet them before you, and that was a very long time ago."

A nagging thought warned her not to go there, but she could not prevent the words from coming out. "And whom was that?"

He was silent for a moment. This was not the time he had planned to tell her about Dorie. Yet, it seemed there would never be a good time, and the subject was raised. He pulled the car off at a deserted picnic area. The entire story of Dorie, the then and the now, came out as matter-of-factly as he could present it. There were no embellishments although he knew just the unfolding of the events raised issues. Is there any right or best way to tell a woman that you love that you possibly might love another?

Celia tried valiantly not to react with any strong emotions. Bailey would have handled it better. She tried to be as mature and reasonable as she could. There was nothing to be happy about the situation except an appreciation of his candor. Nothing would alter her love for him or her desire that they spend their lives together, and she told him so. She would give him as much time and room as he needed to sort out the situation.

He did not change his attitude and behavior towards her over the rest of time they spent together. He was loving and attentive. His working on the book motivated her to do likewise, and the time they were not writing were relaxed and affectionate.

It was not until he left that Cee told Bee the full story. Sensing that Cee was not overly upset, Bee's reaction was subdued. "He is bound to come to his senses. It is not a contest as I see it. I vowed to kill him if he ever makes you unhappy."

"Kill him with kindness. He loves me. I am sure of that. He only needs to be sure of it. I have been patient all of these years waiting for this love. I can wait a bit longer for its total fulfillment. Meanwhile, nothing has changed. We speak, we love, and while I can tell at times he is confused, he makes no secret about wanting and needing me."

"I really have never been in a situation where I had to be as strong as you are, but if I ever am I only hope I can emulate the kind of person you are."

"Bailey and you stand by me. We'll stand by you when and if."

They hugged for a full minute. Celia closed her eyes. The image was clear. Connor was reaching for her outstretched hand.

Writing a book is a honorable, exhausting struggle, like a long bout with a painful illness. One would never undertake such a thing if one were not driven on by some demon whom one can neither resist nor understand.

George Orwell

*How vain it is to sit down and write when
you have not stood up to live.*

Henry David Thoreau

*The life of every man is a diary in which he
means to write one story and writes another;
and his humblest hour is when he compares
the volume as it is with what he vowed to
make it.*

James Matthew Barrie

TWENTY-NINE

The final examination in the freshman class was on the outside readings. There was no examination for the workshop, although the students were asked to voluntarily write a candid critique of the seminar. Connor would consider such comments in formulating an approach for the next semester, and he was looking forward to new students and enhancements for both classes. There were things he wanted to do better, and while he thought the role he played was helpful and inspiring, he knew he could do more.

For the break between semesters he stayed at the University, much to the disappointment of Dorie and Celia. He had kept up a daily long-distance contact with both women since Christmas with no clarification in his mind or certainty in his heart if he had to choose between them. He used as an excuse the driving force to work on the book.

He did spend some time with Kelly, and she was very pleasant to be with. She offered to stay during the break so they could spend some extra time together, but he encouraged her to go home to be with her family which she enjoyed so much. It would have been hurtful to just blurt out that he wanted to be alone.

Being by himself was doing him a great deal of good. While working on the book, it came to him that he could handle his love life as if it were an actual part of the book. It was not far removed from the posed challenge of using in fiction the close proximity of real people and their stories. Knowing full well that each of the three women would wish him to choose one and exclude the others, the option of having all three was not feasible. So, working on the book with that premise, how would it all play out? Would it be possible to reach a conclusion by treating them as characters in the book? Manipulating an intractable reality is an author's prerogative.

The option of not choosing any of them was also impractical. While he still had the basic tenet that he did not need other people, a realistic attainment of happiness and fulfillment meant grasping at a love so close at hand. He dared to surmise that few men had the same wonderful women that were awaiting his decision. He would never have this kind of opportunity again. No doubt, he would not deserve to have such an opportunity again.

So, as the author controlling both the thoughts and actions of all of the characters, he dove into the story headfirst. In the first part of the book he was engrossed in turning fact into fiction. Now, the gears have shifted. A literary involvement to evolve fiction into fact. A dabble in the realm of unrealistic expectations.

Even the order of attention could sway an outcome. He decided that the fairest sequence would be as the women entered his life.

Dorie (the name changed in the book to Laurie) was the first to enter the scene. The main character went to visit Laurie in New York for a weekend. She was receptive to any and all of his overtures. Would making love to her clarify his thinking and feeling? Would it answer doubts about a future for them? Sitting together on the sofa, Laurie kept caressing his arm and leg as she nudged close to him. They kissed, embers of an earlier fire blazing to a warm state. They talked of the old times, laughing heartily at many of the foolish antics they had engaged in. It became highly significant that the emphasis was on looking back and not ahead. Their youthful spirit had guided them in the growing. To love while you are young enables you to love throughout your life. It can be the person, but it is usually the capacity to love. It opens the heart for new impulses and to expand upon feelings implanted in the inner being. It provides the confidence to recognize and hold tight to love.

Over the weekend, the book detailed actions and reactions. Yet, it was that first impression that led him to decide Laurie was not the one. The dilemma then became whether to be honest about it and just tell her or to let her down gradually. He decided to be frank, and she took it better than he thought she would. Maybe she also had concluded that the past was another world. She was young, attractive, and talented. There would be many avenues to travel and many new experiences to evaluate. He need not ever have to worry about her as she had her feet planted solidly on the ground. The parting was friendly, and in spite of promises to stay in touch both knew that this was an ending.

He took Kelly (the name changed in the book to Nellie) to the same restaurant they had gone to on their first date. They talked at length about compatibility and dreams. They touched upon pleasant times shared. The more they spoke, the more they recognized that their relationship was just a special companionship. Each might have wished it to be more than a significant friendship and, perhaps, if time allowed it might have evolved into a more substantive togetherness. The author traced the ebb and flow of the conversation and the emotions. Nellie was a strong woman, a strength bolstered and cushioned by a large and close family. She could handle all of life even if it were by herself.

Did the process of elimination mean that Celia (the name changed to Delia in the book) was the choice by default? He had to be certain.

A visit to Delia raised more problems than it supplied solutions. Her expectation that he live with her in the old family home was logical on her part. Yet, would a big city boy actually be content living in a sleepy little town? Would it eventually bother him that she was a more successful author? Since she was beyond childbearing age, would it be too much of a sacrifice not to have a family? Would the age difference become a hindrance? As a less attractive woman than Laurie or Nellie, would that eventually depress him?

Describing moments of mutual affection and intellectual affinity made him feel better about Delia. Yet, would that be enough to offset the negatives?

In the final analysis it was not about Delia. It rested on what kind of person he was and wanted to be. Was he so trite as to let unimportant things such as looks or age bother him? Could wholesome competition cloud his judgment? Was he so bound by city living as to obscure the true and lasting benefits of small town life? The family of Delia's close friend was as a family of her own, so why would not that suffice for him?

Knowing all that they had in common and that his love for her was strong, the choice became a foregone conclusion. Delia was the woman he wanted to share his life with.

That only leaves reality…………….

***

THIRTY

While the author can control his fiction, reality may elude his intent and design. Others participate in the direction and content of actions. Unanticipated events may alter expectations. Truth may not only be stranger than fiction, it can be totally different.

She could hardly contain her excitement when Connor telephoned that he would like to come and spend the weekend with her. Dorie's wish was coming true. Nostalgia can really spark the renewal of a love interest.

In the back of Connor's mind was the way it played out in the book, and that set the anticipated result. However, when she hugged and kissed him and his nostrils were filled with the clean soap smell of her hair, his resolve evaporated. She was the same idealistic and animated woman he had spent so many meaningful times with. He could not deny that it was wonderful being with her. If he cast aside this form of reality he would be hurting himself as much as her. What was a logical and seemingly effortless course of action in the book promised to be otherwise. Thrown into the mix was his weakness as a man thrust into the arms of a woman who loved him.

Yet, as the weekend progressed, the gist of the book unfolded. Each action and every conversation was steeped in the past. It became a strenuous exercise trying to transform a time long ago into today. The profound observation expressed by Antoine de Saint-Exupery drifted into his mind: *Life has taught us that love does not consist of gazing at each other, but in looking in the same direction.*

On Sunday, her perceptiveness became her reality. "My dear Connor, it just isn't the same, is it? What seemed to be so natural, and what I want to savor again, is a struggle. The world has changed, and it has dragged us along with it. My poems reflect this. From a theme of what was, the words just can't capture what is."

Connor clenched her hand. "Your poetry has always been vibrant because you see and feel more than most people. My eyes have always been wide open. You taught me to look deeply at things and in all directions. Thanks to you, such a quality shows in my writing. I will always be grateful to you. This may sound trite, but I will always love you in a certain way. I can never forget you and what we meant to each other. You taught me to love."

"And you taught me how to live. That is why I was not satisfied with that man I married. That is why I will forge on seeking a satisfaction no less than my poet's heart demands."

'Sounds good to me. I should follow the same course."

"And I will always love you as one loves a memory that has molded character. This new woman must be quite a wonderful person. She is extremely lucky to have you."

An understanding was inherent in their parting embrace. He knew he would send her a copy of each book that he would write. She would share each new poem with him. Part of their past would survive. As he used to read his stories to her and she would offer her poems for his comments, not all would be lost. He felt uplifted when he left.

Dorie was hard-pressed to fully digest all that had happened that weekend. She was not sad about it. He would still occupy a space in her future, although not as she hoped for. She would focus on finding her way with all of the experiences and lessons learned to guide her. She would, as Connor had expressed the concept, forge a passage on each page. If any dark moments emerged, the past could be recalled to furnish a guiding light.

THIRTY-ONE

It had been several days since Kelly had any contact with Connor. She thought of him constantly. There was no denying she loved him. He had every quality she sought in a man, and they were quite compatible. Her longing would have to be held in check. If a friendship was all that she could have with him, that would have to suffice. There is a certain pride in realizing that one is mature and reasonable. Perhaps, it was an offshoot of a scientific approach gained from her sociological training.

His telephone call inviting her out to dinner that Saturday took her by surprise. She was not quite sure how to take it. Was it just a friendly gesture? Did he want to ease the way to tell her that he was going to be with that other woman permanently? Or, was it that he was discerning enough after all to know that she was the most suited for him? She would try to enjoy the date whatever the consequences.

On that Saturday evening, she knew she looked her best in her favorite black dress. Her classic beauty spoke for itself. They dined at the same Italian restaurant they had gone to before, and he appreciated the envious looks from other men as they went to their table. Yet, it was her wit and intelligent conversation that peaked his attraction to her. She was well read in her discipline as well as a host of other subjects. Versed in the ways of people, she had a bearing brimming with confidence and worldliness. He was fascinated listening to her and laughed unabashedly at her humor.

She had agreed to go to dinner with him if they would come back to her place for dessert. Another one of her culinary masterpieces waited. He convinced her to sit on the couch for a while before eating as he was full from the meal.

Kelly was so relaxed she told him many stories of the large family she had, even exclaiming she hoped to have a large family of her own some day. She informed him of the imposing expectancies of her as the oldest child. "One of my sisters is engaged, but she cannot set a wedding date until after I marry. I feel sorry for her. I have thought of concocting a story that I am gay to break the unwritten rule. They would never buy it."

"Little wonder. That is too farfetched even for me to believe. Your man will come along, I am sure. A treasure can be hidden for just so long."

"I hope so. I am too smart and combative for most men. A man should not feel threatened by such qualities. The way I look at it, they might come in handy."

"I should say so."

"Do I scare you?"

"Only in overfeeding me."

"I'll just let you have one slice of the cocoanut custard pie waiting in the kitchen."

"Let's not carry this to extremes, please."

She sure had a lovely smile. He leaned in and took her in his arms and the kiss was warm and tantalizing. They kissed again.

"That's my kind of dessert," she whispered. "But, unlike you, I would like more, please."

"Glad to oblige."

The ensuing kisses were passionate. She led him up to the bedroom where the feeling of love that enfolded them was consummated. She was ecstatic. He was more confused than ever. How could he stray so far from the book?

THIRTY-TWO

Connor's parents were also perplexed. He stopped to see them before going to Celia's home. He told them that he was now certain that he was in love with a woman other than the one he had brought to meet them. Adding to the uncertainty was that he had not yet told that woman of this development. He explained she was a Sociology professor at the University. As much as he enjoyed writing, he loved teaching and planned on staying there to teach. They would teach there together. His parents assured him that everything would work out even though they were not sure they understood it all.

Celia had talked it over with Bailey, and it was easily deduced that Connor's feelings had changed. There were no longer the daily telephone conversations. When he did call, he was friendly enough but the outpourings of love were absent. Upon his arrival, his embrace was half-hearted. Bailey whispered in her ear, "Be strong. His heart has changed."

She did not need Bailey's confirmation of what her woman's sense combined with her author's insight had already told her. What other choice did she have but to accept it? There was really no way to fight it. The biggest problem might be how to prevent Becca from killing him.

He was kind in the telling of it all, and while she expected nothing less from him it did confirm that one of his loving characteristics was his display of consideration. It tore her heart apart. She tried to be gentle and caring with him. She wished him a wonderful life and vowed to always love him. If things changed, she and Bailey would still be here.

After he left, Cee went to Bee's studio and told her it all. There were lots of tears, many hugs, as well as numerous understanding and consoling words. By the end of the discussion, Cee did not feel so downtrodden. Bee was a wonderful friend, and that situation served to salve the unpleasant turn of events. As she explained to Bee, she had her moment of love, a moment that she might never have had. It would be a lasting and warm memory. She was sure it would also serve as an inspiration in writing books, propelling Bailey to new challenges and exciting adventures. She downplayed that Connor decided to stay on teaching and that he did not want to uproot her from her good life. She would have done that for love, but she would be giving up a great deal. A conflict between two forms of happiness might well be unsettling.

A mixture of emotions flooded over Connor as drove back to Blantyre. He felt badly about Celia, but he was sure her staunch mannerism and close friendship with Becca would pull her through as well as with any other adverse situation that might arise. He also felt a building excitement about the certain love he had for Kelly. It would be most fulfilling having a partner from a different discipline, one who was energetic, bright, and supportive. He would like to be all of that for her as well. He felt they would have a wonderful life together, and he looked forward to having the large family she desired.

When Kelly opened the door in response to the ring of the doorbell, he quickly stepped inside and kissed her fervently. "Your sister sent me to marry you. I love you on my own."

www.ingramcontent.com/pod-product-compliance
Lightning Source LLC
Chambersburg PA
CBHW020731210626
46807CB00016B/1239